The Castle *of* Crossed Destinies

Books by Italo Calvino

The Baron in the Trees
The Nonexistent Knight *and* The Cloven Viscount
The Path to the Nest of Spiders
Cosmicomics
t zero
The Watcher and Other Stories
Invisible Cities
The Castle of Crossed Destinies
Italian Folktales
If on a winter's night a traveler
Marcovaldo, or The seasons in the city
Difficult Loves
Mr. Palomar
The Uses of Literature
Under the Jaguar Sun
Six Memos for the Next Millennium
Road to San Giovanni

Italo Calvino

The Castle
of Crossed
Destinies

Translated from the Italian by William Weaver

A Harvest Book
A Helen and Kurt Wolff Book
Harcourt, Inc.
Orlando Austin New York San Diego London

www.HarcourtBooks.com

Pages 3 through 48 originally appeared in Italo
Calvino's *Tarots: The Visconti Pack in Bergamo
and New York,* published by Franco Maria Ricci
editore and distributed in the United States by
Rizzoli International Publications, Inc., New York, 1976.

Library of Congress Cataloging-in-Publication Data
Calvino, Italo.
    Translation of Il castello dei destini incrociati.
    "A Helen and Kurt Wolff book."
    The castle of crossed destinies.
    "A Harvest book."
    I. Title.
PZ3.CI3956Cas 1979 [PQ4809.A45] 853'.9'14 78-23588
ISBN 978-0-15-615455-0 (Harvest pbk.)

Text type set in Ehrhardt
Printed in the United States of America

DOC 30 29 28 27 26 25 24 23 22 21

Contents

The Castle of Crossed Destinies

The Castle

In the midst of a thick forest, there was a castle that gave shelter to all travelers overtaken by night on their journey: lords and ladies, royalty and their retinue, humble wayfarers.

I crossed a rattling drawbridge. I slipped from my saddle in a dark courtyard. Silent grooms took my horse. I was breathless, hardly able to stand on my legs; after entering the forest I had faced so many trials, encounters, apparitions, duels, that I could no longer order my actions or my thoughts.

I climbed some stairs; I found myself in a high, spacious hall. Many people—also transient guests surely, who had preceded me along the path through the woods —were seated at supper at a table lighted by candelabra.

As I looked around, I felt a curious sensation, or, rather, two distinct sensations, which mingled in my mind, still upset and somewhat unstable in my weariness. I seemed to be at a sumptuous court, which no one would have expected to find in such a rustic and out-of-the-way castle; and its wealth was evident not only in the costly furnishings and the graven vessels, but also in the calm and ease which reigned among those at the table, all handsome of person and clothed with elaborate elegance. But, at the same time, I remarked a feeling of random, of disorder, if not actually of license, as if this were not a lordly dwelling but an inn of passage, where people unknown to one another live together for one night and where, in that enforced promiscuity, all feel a relaxation of the rules by which they live in their own surroundings, and—as one resigns oneself to less comfortable ways of life—so one also indulges in freer, unfamiliar behavior. In fact, the two contradictory impressions could nevertheless refer to a single object: whether the castle, for years visited only as a stopping place, had gradually degenerated into an inn, and the lord and his lady had found themselves reduced to the roles of host and hostess, though still going through the motions of their aristocratic hospitality; or whether a tavern, such as one often sees in the vicinity of castles, to give drink to soldiers and horsemen, had invaded—the castle being long abandoned—the ancient, noble halls to install its benches and hogsheads there, and the pomp of those rooms—as well as the coming and going of illustrious customers—had conferred on the inn an unforeseen dignity, sufficient to put ideas in the heads of the host and hostess, who finally came to believe themselves the rulers of a brilliant court.

These thoughts, to tell the truth, occupied me only for a moment; stronger were my relief at being safe and sound in the midst of a select company and my impatience to strike up a conversation (at a nod of invitation from the man who seemed the lord—or the host—I had sat down at the only empty place) and to exchange with my traveling companions tales of the adventures we had undergone. But at this table, contrary to the custom of inns, and also of courts, no one uttered a word. When a guest wished to ask his neighbor to pass the salt or the ginger, he did so with a gesture, and with gestures he also addressed the servants, motioning them to cut him a slice of pheasant pie or to pour him a half pint of wine.

I decided to break what I believed a drowsiness of tongues after the trials of the journey, and I was about to burst forth with a loud exclamation such as "Health to all!" or "Well met!" or "It's an ill wind . . ."; but no sound came from my lips. The drumming of spoons, the rattle of goblets and crockery were enough to persuade me I had not gone deaf: I could only presume I had been struck dumb. My fellow diners confirmed this supposition, moving their lips silently in a gracefully resigned manner: it was clear that crossing the forest had cost each of us the power of speech.

When our supper ended in a muteness which the sounds of chewing and the smacking of lips gulping wine did not make more pleasant, we remained seated, looking one another in the face, with the torment of not being able to exchange the many experiences each of us had to communicate. At that point, on the table which had just been cleared, the man who seemed the lord of the castle set a pack of playing cards. They were tarot cards, larger than the kind we use for ordinary games or that gypsies employ for predicting the future, but it was possible to discern more or less the same figures that are painted in the enamels of the most precious miniatures. Kings, Queens, Knights, and Pages were all young people magnificently dressed, as if for a princely feast; the twenty-two Major Arcana seemed the tapestries of a court theater; and cups, coins, swords, clubs shone like heraldic devices adorned with scrolls and arabesques.

We began to spread out the cards on the table, face up, and to give them their proper value in games, or their true meaning in the reading of fortunes. And yet none of us seemed to wish to begin playing, and still less to question the future, since we were as if drained of all future, suspended in a journey that had not ended nor was to end. There was something else we saw in those tarots, something that no longer allowed us to take our eyes from the gilded pieces of that mosaic.

One of the guests drew the scattered cards to himself, leaving a large part of the table clear; but he did not gather them into a pack nor did he shuffle them; he took one card and placed it in front of himself. We all noticed the resemblance between his face and the face on the card, and we thought we understood that, with the card, he wanted to say "I" and that he was preparing to tell his story.

The Tale of the Ingrate
and His Punishment

Introducing himself to us with the figure of the *Knight of Cups*—a pink and blond youth displaying a sun-shaped cloak radiant with embroidery, and offering with outstretched hand a gift like those of the Magi—our fellow guest probably wished to inform us of his wealthy station, his inclination toward luxury and prodigality, and also—showing himself mounted—his spirit of adventure, inspired, however (I judged, observing all that embroidery, even on the steed's trappings), more by a love of display than by a true knightly vocation.

The handsome youth made a gesture, as if to demand our full attention, and then began his silent tale, arranging three cards in a row on the table: the *King of Coins*, the *Ten of Coins*, and the *Nine of Clubs*. The mournful expression with which he set down the first of these cards, and the joyous look with which he showed the next one, seemed to want to tell us that, his father having died—the *King of Coins* represented a slightly older personage than the others, with a mature and prosperous appearance—he had come into possession of a considerable fortune and had immediately set forth on his travels. This last notion we de-

duced from his arm's movement in throwing down the *Nine of Clubs*, which—with the tangle of boughs extended over a sparse growth of leaves and little wild flowers—reminded us of the forest through which we had recently passed. (Indeed, if one examined the card with a sharper eye, the vertical line, which crosses the other, oblique pieces of wood, suggested, in fact, the idea of the road penetrating into the depth of the forest.)

This, then, could be the beginning of the story: the knight, as soon as he learned he had the means to shine at the most magnificent courts, hastened to set out, his purse brimming with gold coins, to visit the most famous castles of the neighboring country, perhaps with the aim of winning a wife of high degree; and cherishing these dreams, he entered the woods.

To this row of cards, another was added, which surely announced some ugly encounter: *Strength*. In our tarot pack this Arcanum was represented by an armed brute, whose evil intentions were unequivocally indicated by his cruel expression, by the club swung in the air, and by his violence in striking a lion to the ground with a single sharp blow, as one might kill a rabbit. The story was, alas, clear: in the heart of the forest the knight was ambushed by a fierce brigand. Our worst prophecies were confirmed by the following card, the Twelfth Arcanum, known as *The Hanged Man*, in which you see a man in shirt and trousers, strung up by one foot, his head hanging downward. In the man we again recognized our blond youth; the brigand had stripped him of all his belongings and had left him hanging from a branch, his head toward the ground.

We sighed in relief at the news given us by the Arcanum *Temperance*, set on the table by our companion with an expression of gratitude. From it we learned that the hanging man had heard footsteps approaching and his upside-down eye had seen a maiden, daughter perhaps of a woodsman or a goatherd, who was advancing, her calves bare, over the meadows, carrying two pitchers of water, surely on her way back from the spring. We had no doubt that the man strung up by his feet would be freed and restored to his natural position by that simple child of the woods. When we saw the *Ace of Cups* fall, with its depiction of a fountain purling amidst flowering mosses and rustling wings, we could almost hear the gurgle of a nearby spring and the gasping of that man, lying prone to quench his thirst.

But there are fountains—as some of us surely thought —that, once you drink from them, increase your thirst instead of slaking it. One might predict that between the two young people there sprang up, once the knight recovered from his dizziness, a sentiment that went beyond gratitude (on his part) and beyond pity (on hers), and that this sentiment would find—thanks to the woods' complicity and darkness—prompt expression in an embrace on the grassy meadow. It was no accident that the next card was a *Two of Cups*, embellished with a scroll reading "My Love" and bedecked with forget-me-nots: a more than probable indication of an amorous encounter.

All of us, and especially the ladies of the company, were preparing to enjoy the continuation of a tender love story, when the knight laid down another *Club*, the *Seven*, where, among the dark trunks of a forest, we

seemed to see his faint shadow moving away. There was no deceiving ourselves that matters had gone otherwise: the sylvan idyll had been brief, poor maiden; having plucked the flower in the meadow and dropped it there, the ungrateful knight did not even look back to bid her farewell.

At this point it was clear that a second part of the tale was beginning, perhaps after a lapse of time. The narrator, in fact, had begun arranging other cards in a new row, beside the first, on the left; he set down two cards, *The Empress* and the *Eight of Cups*. The sudden change of scene disconcerted us for a moment; but the solution quickly asserted itself, I believe to us all, and it was that the knight had finally found what he had been seeking, a wealthy bride of high lineage, such as we saw depicted there, a crowned head, indeed, with her family shield and her insipid face—also slightly older than he, as the more malicious amongst us surely noticed—in a dress all embroidered in linked rings as if to say, "Marry me, marry me." An invitation promptly accepted, since the *Cups* card suggested a wedding banquet, with two rows of guests toasting the couple at the end of the festooned table.

The card that was laid down next, the *Knight of Swords,* appearing in war array, announced an unforeseen event: either a mounted messenger had burst in on the feast, bearing disturbing news, or the groom himself had abandoned the wedding banquet to hasten, armed, into the woods at some mysterious summons, or perhaps both things at once: the groom had been informed of a sudden apparition and had immediately seized his arms and leapt into the saddle. (The wiser for his past adventure, he never stuck his nose out of the door unless armed from head to toe.)

Impatiently, we awaited a more explanatory card; and *The Sun* then came. The painter had depicted the day's star in the hands of a child, running or, rather, flying over a vast and varied landscape. The interpretation of this passage in the tale was not easy. It could simply mean "it was a fine sunny day," and in this case our narrator was wasting his cards telling us inessential details. But perhaps the allegorical significance of the picture was less to be dwelt on than its literal meaning: a half-naked child had been seen running in the neighborhood of the castle where the wedding was being celebrated, and the groom had deserted the banquet to pursue that urchin.

The object the child was carrying, however, could not be overlooked: that radiant head might contain the solution to the riddle. Glancing again at the card with which our hero had first introduced himself, we were reminded of the solar patterns or embroidered motifs on the cloak he had been wearing when attacked by the brigand: perhaps that cloak, which the knight had forgotten in the meadow of his fleeting love, had been fluttering over the countryside like a kite, and he was pursuing the urchin to recover it, or else out of curiosity to know how it had ended up there, what link, in other words, connected the cloak, the child, and the maiden of the forest.

We hoped these questions would be answered by the following card, and when we saw it was *Justice* we were convinced that in this Arcanum—which showed not only a woman with sword and scales, as in ordinary tarot packs, but also, in the background (or, according

to how you looked at it, in a lunette over the main figure) a mounted warrior (or an Amazon?), in armor, moving to the attack—there was contained one of the chapters richest in adventures of our tale. We could only venture some guesses. For example: as he was about to overtake the child with the kite, the pursuer had found his way blocked by another knight, fully armed. What can they have said to each other? To begin with: "Who goes there?"

And the unknown knight then revealed his countenance, the face of a woman our companion recognized as the maiden who had saved him in the forest, now fuller, more resolute, and more calm, with the hint of a melancholy smile on her lips. "What do you want of me?" he must have asked her then.

"Justice!" the Amazon said. (The scales, in fact, alluded to this answer.)

On further reflection, however, we thought the encounter might have gone as follows: a mounted Amazon came charging from the woods (background or lunette figure) and shouted at him: "Halt! Do you know whom you are pursuing?"

"Who, pray?"

"Your son!" the warrior-woman said, revealing her face (the figure in the foreground).

"What can I do?" our hero must have asked, gripped by sudden and belated remorse.

"Face the justice (*scales*) of God! Defend yourself!" and she (*sword*) brandished her sword.

"Now he'll tell us about the duel," I thought, and, to be sure, the card thrown down at that moment was the clattering *Two of Swords*. The shredded leaves of the woods flew and the climbing vines twisted around the two blades. But the disconsolate gaze that the narrator cast at this card left no uncertainty as to the outcome: his adversary proved to be a seasoned swordswoman; so it was his turn, now, to lie bleeding in the midst of the meadow.

He comes to his senses, opens his eyes, and what does he see? (This was the narrator's miming—a bit overdone, to tell the truth—inviting us to wait for the next card as if for a revelation.) *The Popess*, mysterious, nun-like crowned figure. Had he been given succor by a female monarch? His eyes, staring at the card, were filled with horror. A witch? He raised his imploring hands in a gesture of devout terror. The High Priestess of a secret and sanguinary cult?

"Know then that, in the person of that maiden, you have offended"—(what else can the Popess have said to him, to cause that grimace of terror?)—"you have offended Cybele, the goddess to whom this forest is sacred. Now you have fallen into our hands."

And what can he have replied, except, in an imploring stammer: "I shall expiate, I shall appease, mercy. . . ."

"Now the forest shall have you. The forest is self-loss, mingling. To join us you must lose yourself, tear away your attributes, dismember yourself, be transformed into the undistinguished, join the swarm of Maenads who run screaming in the woods."

"No!" was the cry we saw escape his silenced throat, but already the last card was concluding his tale, and this was the *Eight of Swords*, the sharp blades of Cybele's disheveled followers, as they fell upon him and tore him to pieces.

THE TALE OF THE INGRATE

The Tale of the Alchemist
Who Sold His Soul

The emotion aroused by this story had not yet died away when another of our companions indicated that he wanted to tell his own. One episode, especially, in the knight's tale seemed to have attracted his attention, or, rather, it was one of the random pairings of cards in the second row: the *Ace of Cups*, placed beside *The Popess*. To suggest how he felt personally involved in that juxtaposition, he pushed up to the right of those two cards the figure of the *King of Cups* (which could have passed for a very youthful and—to tell the truth—exaggeratedly flattering portrait of him) and, on the left, continuing in a horizontal line, an *Eight of Clubs*.

The first interpretation that this sequence called to mind, if we continued attributing an aura of voluptuousness to the fountain, was that our fellow guest had had amorous relations with a nun in a wood. Or else that he had offered her copious drink, since the fountain, if you examined it closely, seemed to pour from a little cask set on top of a grape press. But the melancholy stare of the man's face seemed lost in speculations from which not only carnal passions but even the most venial pleasures of table and cellar had to be excluded. Lofty meditations must have been his, though his

worldly appearance left no doubt that they were still addressed to the Earth and not to Heaven. (And so another possible interpretation was eliminated: that the card depicted a holy-water stoup.)

The most probable hypothesis that occurred to me was that the card stood for the Fountain of Life, the supreme goal of the alchemist's search, and that our companion was, in fact, one of those scholars who scrutinize alembics and crucibles (like the complicated vessel that his royally clad figure held in its hand), trying to wrest from Nature her secrets, and especially that of the transformation of metals.

We could believe that, from his earliest youth (this was the meaning of the portrait with adolescent features, which could at the same time allude also to the elixir of long life) he had had no other passion (the fountain remained nevertheless an amorous symbol) save the manipulation of the elements, and for years he had waited to see the yellow king of the mineral world precipitate in the depths of his cauldron. And in this quest he had finally sought the counsel and aid of those women sometimes encountered in forests, experts in philters and magic potions, devoted to the arts of witchcraft and foretelling the future (like the woman he indicated, with superstitious reverence, as *The Popess*).

The card that came next, *The Emperor,* could naturally refer to a prophecy of the forest witch: You will become the most powerful man in the world.

It would hardly have been surprising if our alchemist had got a swelled head, expecting any day an extraordinary change in the course of his life. This event must have been indicated in the following card, which was the enigmatic First Arcanum, sometimes known as *The Juggler*, in which some see a charlatan or magician performing his tricks.

So, then, our hero, raising his eyes from his desk, had seen a magician seated before him, as he handled his alembics and his retorts.

"Who are you? What are you doing here?"

"Watch what I do," the magician answered, pointing to a glass flask over a fire.

The dazzled look with which our companion threw down the *Seven of Coins* left no doubt about what he had seen: the splendor of all the mines of the Orient lying open before him.

"You can give me the secret of gold?" he must have asked the charlatan.

The following card was a *Two of Coins*, sign of an exchange, I thought spontaneously, a sale, a barter.

"I will sell it to you!" the unknown visitor must have replied.

"What do you want in return?"

The answer we all expected was "Your soul!" but we were not sure until the narrator turned over the new card (and he lingered a moment before doing so, not placing it next to the previous one but after the last, thus beginning a new row in the opposite direction). This card was *The Devil*; in short, he had recognized in the charlatan the old prince of all mingling and ambiguity—just as we now recognized our companion as Doctor Faust.

So Mephistopheles had then answered, "Your soul!": an idea that can be represented only with the figure of Psyche, the young girl who illuminates the shadows

with her light, as she is contemplated in *The Star*. The *Five of Cups* which was then shown us could be read as the alchemistic secret the Devil revealed to Faust, or as a toast to seal their bargain, or as the bells which, with their strokes, put the infernal visitor to flight. But we could also interpret the card as a discourse upon the soul and upon the body as the soul's vessel. (One of the five cups was painted horizontally, as if it were empty.)

"My soul?" our Faust may have answered. "And what if I had no soul?"

But perhaps it was not for an individual soul that Mephistopheles had inconvenienced himself. "With the gold you will build a city," he was saying to Faust. "It is the entire city's soul that I want in exchange."

"It's a deal."

And the Devil could then truly vanish with a sneer that seemed a howl: long-time inhabitant of steeples, accustomed to contemplating, from his perch on a rainspout, the expanse of roofs, he knew that the souls of cities are more substantial and more lasting than those of all their inhabitants put together.

Now there was still *The Wheel of Fortune* to interpret, one of the most complicated images in the whole tarot game. It could mean simply that fortune had turned in Faust's direction, but this explanation seemed too obvious for the alchemist's narrative style, always elliptical and allusive. On the other hand, it was legitimate to suppose that our doctor, having got possession of the diabolical secret, conceived a monstrous plan: to change into gold all that was changeable. The wheel of the Tenth Arcanum would then literally mean the toiling gears of the Great Gold Mill, the gigantic mechanism which would raise up the Metropolis of Precious Metal; and the human forms of various ages seen pushing the wheel or rotating with it were there to indicate the crowds of men who eagerly lent a hand to the project and dedicated the years of their lives to turning those wheels day and night. This interpretation failed to take into account all the details of the miniature (for example, the animalesque ears and tails that adorned some of the revolving human figures), but it was a basis for interpreting the following cards of cups and coins as the Kingdom of Abundance in which the City of Gold's inhabitants wallowed. (The rows of yellow circles perhaps evoked the gleaming domes of golden skyscrapers that flanked the streets of the Metropolis.)

But when would the established price be collected by the Cloven Contracting Party? The story's two final cards were already on the table, placed there by the first narrator: the *Two of Swords* and *Temperance*. At the gates of the City of Gold armed guards blocked the way to anyone who wished to enter, to prevent access to the Cloven-hooved Collector, no matter in what guise he might turn up. And even if a simple maiden, like the one in the last card, were to approach, the guards made her halt.

"You lock your gates in vain"—this was the answer that could be expected from the water-bearer. "I take care not to enter a City where all is of solid metal. We who live in what is fluid visit only elements that flow and mingle."

Was she a water nymph? Was she the queen of the elves of the air? An angel of the liquid fire in the earth's center?

(In *The Wheel of Fortune,* if you looked carefully, the bestial metamorphoses seemed perhaps only the first step in a regression of the human to the vegetable and mineral.)

"Are you afraid our souls will fall into the Devil's hands?" those of the City must have asked.

"No, for you have no soul to give him."

The Tale of the Doomed Bride

I have no idea how many of us managed to decipher the tale somehow, without getting lost among all those low cards, cups and coins, that popped up just when we were most eager for a clear exposition of the facts. The narrator's powers of communication were scant, perhaps because his genius was more inclined to the severity of abstractions than to the obviousness of images. In any case, some of us allowed our minds to wander, or we lingered over certain couplings of cards and were unable to go on.

One of us, for example, a warrior with melancholy eyes, began toying with a *Page of Swords*, which strongly resembled him, and a *Six of Clubs*; and he placed them beside the *Seven of Coins* and *The Star*, as if he wanted to build up a vertical row on his own.

Perhaps for him, a soldier lost in the woods, those cards, followed by *The Star*, meant a glimmer, like a will-o'-the wisp's, which had drawn him to a clearing among the trees, where a young maiden of starry pallor appeared to him, wandering in the night in her shift, her hair undone, holding a lighted taper aloft.

However it was, he continued unperturbed, making his vertical line; he put down two *Swords*, a *Seven* and

a *Queen*, a combination difficult to interpret as such. It required perhaps a bit of dialogue, instead, along these lines:

"Noble knight, I implore you, remove your weapons and your breastplate, and let me put them on!" (In the miniature, the *Queen of Swords* wears a set of armor, complete with tasses, couters, gauntlets, which shows like an iron undergarment below the embroidered hems of her snow-white silken sleeves.) "In a daze, I promised myself to someone whose embrace I now abhor, and tonight he will come to demand I keep my word! I can hear him approaching! If I am armed, he cannot clasp me! Pray, save a persecuted maiden!"

There was no doubt that the warrior had promptly consented. With the armor on, the poor maid was transformed into a tourney queen, strutting, preening. A smile of sensual joy kindled the pallor of her face.

But here again a whole assortment of stupid cards began, and it was a problem to make head or tail of them: a *Two of Clubs* (sign of a crossroads, a choice?), an *Eight of Coins* (hidden treasure?), a *Six of Cups* (an amorous tryst?).

"Your courtesy deserves a guerdon," the woman of the forest must have said. "Choose the prize you prefer: I can give you riches, or . . ."

"Or?"

". . . I can give you myself."

The warrior's hand tapped the *Cups* card: he had chosen love.

For the rest of the tale we had to use our imagination: he was already naked, she stripped off the armor she had barely put on, and among the bronze scales our hero grasped a round and taut and soft breast, he slipped between the iron cuisse and the warm thigh. . . .

Reserved and modest by nature, the soldier did not dwell on the details: he told us what he could by putting beside the *Cups* card another gilded *Coins* card, with a wistful look, as if to exclaim: "I thought I had entered Paradise. . . ."

The card he set down afterward confirmed this image of the threshold of Paradise, but at the same time it brusquely interrupted his voluptuous abandon: it was *The Pope*, a pontiff with an austere white beard, like the first Pope, now guardian of the Gate of Heaven.

"Who dares speak of Paradise?" High over the forest, in the midst of the sky, Saint Peter appeared, enthroned, thundering: "For her our gates are closed to all eternity!"

The way our narrator put down a new card, rapidly, but keeping it hidden and shielding his eyes with his other hand, prepared us for a revelation: the one he had found when, lowering his gaze from the menacing threshold of Heaven, he looked at the lady in whose arms he was lying, and saw that the gorget no longer framed a turtle-dove countenance, pert dimples, little tilted nose, but an array of teeth without gums or lips, two nostrils hollowed from bone, the yellow jaws of a skull, and he felt his limbs entwined with the stiff limbs of a corpse.

The ghastly sight of Arcanum Thirteen (the legend *Death* does not even appear in the decks whose major cards bear their names written out) aroused in all of us an impatience to learn the rest of the tale. Was the *Ten of Swords* which now came the barrier of archangels, blocking the damned soul's access to Heaven? Was

Il Diavolo

the *Five of Clubs* announcing a path through the forest?

At this point the file of cards was again connected with *The Devil,* already set in that place by the previous narrator.

I did not have to rack my brains long to understand that from the forest had come the betrothed whom the deceased bride-to-be had so feared: Beelzebub in person, who exclaimed: "So, my proud beauty, here is an end to your shifting your cards! I care not twopence (*Two of Coins*) for all your arms and armor (*Four of Swords*)!" And, with that, he carried her down into the bowels of the earth.

A Grave-Robber's Tale

The cold sweat was still damp on my spine when I was already obliged to follow another neighbor, in whom the quadrangle of *Death, Pope, Eight of Coins, Two of Clubs* seemed to waken other memories, to judge by the way his gaze shifted about, while he bent his head to one side, as if uncertain from which direction to enter the square. When he set at its edge the *Page of Coins*, a figure in which it was easy to recognize his provocative, bold manner, I knew he also wanted to tell us something, beginning there, and I knew it was his own story.

But what did this carefree youth have in common with the macabre reign of skeletons evoked by Arcanum Thirteen? He surely was not the sort to roam meditating in graveyards, unless he had been drawn there by some rascally intention: for example, to force the graves and steal from the dead the precious objects they had rashly taken with them on their last journey. . . .

It is usually the Great of the Earth who are buried with the attributes of their rule, gold crowns, rings, scepters, garments of shining metal. If this young man was really a grave-robber, he must have gone to cemeteries in search of the most illustrious graves, the tomb

of a *Pope*, for example, since pontiffs descend into their graves in all the splendor of their trappings. The thief, on a moonless night, must have raised the heavy lid of the tomb, with *Two Clubs* as levers, and then dropped into the sepulcher.

And after that? The narrator set an *Ace of Clubs* down and made an upward gesture, as of something growing: for a moment I thought my whole conjecture was mistaken, that gesture seemed so contradictory to the thief's sinking into the papal tomb. Unless I was to suppose that, as soon as the tomb was uncovered, a tree trunk, erect and very tall, appeared, and that the thief climbed up it, or else he felt himself borne up, to the top of the tree, among the branches, into the leafy crown.

The man may have been a gallows bird, but luckily, in telling his tale he did not simply confine himself to adding one tarot to another (he proceeded with pairs of flanking cards, in a double horizontal row, from left to right); he aided himself with well-calculated gesticulation, simplifying our task a bit. And so I managed to understand that, with the *Ten of Cups*, he meant the sight of the cemetery from above, as he contemplated it from the top of the tree, with all the tombs lined up on their pedestals along the paths. Whereas with the Arcanum known as *The Angel* or *The Last Judgment* (in which the angels around the celestial throne are sounding the reveille that uncovers the tombs) he perhaps wanted only to underline the fact that he was looking down on the tombs from above as the inhabitants of Heaven might on the Great Day.

At the top of the tree, climbing up like an urchin, our

hero reached a suspended city. Or so I interpreted the greatest of the Arcana, *The World,* which in this tarot pack depicts a city floating on waves or clouds and held up by two winged cherubs. It was a city whose roofs touched heaven's vault, as *The Tower* of Babel once had, as we were shown, next, by another Arcanum.

"He who descends into the abyss of Death and climbs again the Tree of Life"—these are the words with which I imagined our involuntary pilgrim was received—"arrives in the City of the Possible, from which the Whole is contemplated and Choices are decided."

Here the narrator's miming no longer assisted us and we had to work again through conjectures. We could imagine that, having entered the City of the Whole and of the Parts, our scoundrel heard himself addressed with these words:

"Do you want riches (*Coins*) or power (*Swords*) or wisdom (*Cups*)? Choose, at once!"

It was a stern and radiant archangel (*Knight of Swords*) who addressed this question to him, and our hero answered quickly, crying out: "I choose riches (*Coins*)!"

"You shall have *Clubs!*" was the reply of the mounted archangel, as city and tree dissolved into smoke and the thief hurtled down through crashing, broken branches into the midst of the forest.

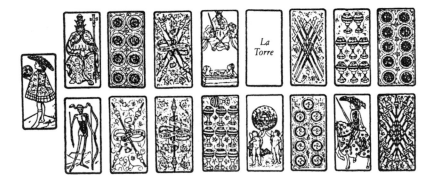

The Tale of Roland Crazed with Love

Now the cards arranged on the table formed a square, with all of its sides closed, and a still-empty window left in the center. Over this empty space bent one of the guests, who until then had seemed lost in thought, his gaze wandering. He was a gigantic warrior; he raised his arms as if they were of lead, and he turned his head slowly as if the heavy burden of his thoughts had cracked his spine. Certainly a profound distress was weighing upon this captain who, not long ago, must have been like murderous lightning in warfare.

He set down the figure of the *King of Swords*, which attempted to render in a single portrait his bellicose past and his melancholy present, at the square's left edge, beside the *Ten of Swords*. And our eyes seemed suddenly blinded by the great dust cloud of battles: we heard the blare of trumpets; already the shattered spears were flying; already the clashing horses' muzzles were drenched in iridescent foam; already the swords, with the flat or the cutting edge, were striking against the flat or cutting edge of other swords; and where a circle of living enemies sprang up in their saddles and then, falling again, found not their horses but the grave, there in the center of this circle was the paladin Roland, whirl-

ing his Durendal. We had recognized him; it was he, telling his own story, in fits and starts, pressing his iron-like finger on each card.

Now he pointed to the *Queen of Swords*. In the figure of this blond woman who, among sharpened blades and iron plates, proffers the elusive smile of a sensual game, we recognized Angelica, the enchantress come from Cathay to ruin the French armies; and we were convinced Count Roland was still in love with her.

After her came the empty space: Roland put a card there, the *Ten of Clubs*. We saw the forest open, reluctantly, at the champion's progress, the needles of the fir trees bristle like a porcupine's quills, the oaks swell their trunks' muscular chests, the beeches tear their roots from the ground to block his progress. The whole wood seemed to say to him: "Go no farther! Why are you deserting the metallic fields of war, realm of the discontinuous and the distinct, the congenial massacres where your talent excels in sundering and excluding, to venture now into green, mucilaginous Nature, among the coils of living continuity? The forest of love, Roland, is no place for you! You are pursuing an enemy from whose snares no shield can protect you. Forget Angelica! Turn back!"

But it was certain that Roland did not lend an ear to these warnings and a single vision held him: the one represented by Arcanum Seven, which he now put on the table, *The Chariot*. The artist who, with gleaming enamels, had illuminated these tarots of ours had this *Chariot* driven not by the usual king seen in more common cards, but by a woman dressed as a sorceress or Oriental queen, holding the reins of two white, winged

horses. This was how Roland's raving imagination conceived Angelica's enchanted entrance into the forest; it
was a print of flying hoofs he pursued, lighter than a
butterfly's feet, the trail that was his guide through the
thicket.

Wretched man! He did not yet know that in the deepest part of the thicket Angelica and Medoro were meanwhile united in a soft, heart-rending embrace. It took
the Arcanum of *Love* to reveal this to him, with the
languor of desire our miniaturist had been able to give
the two lovers' gaze. (We began to understand that,
with those iron hands and that dreaming air, Roland
had, from the beginning, kept for himself the most beautiful cards in the pack, allowing the others to stammer
out their vicissitudes to the sound of cups and clubs,
gold coins and swords.)

The truth forced its way into Roland's thoughts: in
the moist depths of the female forest there is a temple of
Eros where other values count, not the ones determined
by his Durendal. Angelica's favorite was not one of the
illustrious commanders of troops but a youth of the en-
tourage, slender, coy as a girl; his figure, enlarged, appeared in the following card: the *Page of Clubs*.

Where had the lovers fled? Whichever path they had
taken, the substance they were made of was too fragile
and elusive to allow the paladin's iron paws to grasp
them. When he had lost all uncertainty about the end of
his hopes, Roland made a few clumsy gestures—drawing his sword, digging in his spurs, stiffening his legs in
his stirrups—and then something in him broke, shattered, exploded, melted: all of a sudden the light of his
intellect was extinguished; he was left in darkness.

Now the bridge of cards drawn across the square touched the opposite side, at the level of *The Sun*. A cupid in flight was carrying off Roland's sanity, and he hovered over the land of France challenged by the Infidels, over the sea which Saracen galleys would ply with impunity, now that Christianity's stoutest champion lay beclouded by madness.

Force ended the row. I shut my eyes. My heart could not bear the sight of that flower of chivalry transformed into a blind telluric explosion, like a cyclone or an earthquake. As the Moslem hordes had once been mowed down by Durendal, now the whirling of his club felled the fierce beasts that from Africa through the decay of the invasions had passed to the coasts of Provence and Catalonia; a cloak of feline pelts, tawny and striped and spotted, would cover the fields, now become deserts, where he passed: nor would the cautious lion, nor the linear tiger, nor the retractile leopard survive the slaughter. Then it would be the turn of the elephant, the rhinoceros, and the river-horse or hippopotamus: a layer of pachyderm skins was about to thicken on callused, arid Europe.

The narrator's iron, punctilious finger made a paragraph, or, rather, it began to spell out the line below, starting at the left. I saw (and heard) the crash of the oaks uprooted by the maniac in the *Five of Clubs*, and I regretted the idleness of Durendal, hung on a tree and forgotten in the *Seven of Swords*, I deplored the waste of energy and wealth in the *Five of Coins* (added, for the occasion, in the empty space).

The card he now placed there in the middle was *The Moon*. A cold gleam shines on the dark Earth. A nymph with a mad look raises her hand to the golden celestial sickle as if she were playing the harp. True, the string hangs broken from her bow: the Moon is a defeated planet, and the conquering Earth is the Moon's prisoner. Roland races over an Earth that is now lunar.

The card of *The Fool*, displayed immediately afterward, was all the more eloquent on the subject. Now that the greatest knot of fury had been undone, with the club on his shoulder like a fishing pole, thin as a skull, tattered, without trousers, his head full of feathers (all sorts of things were stuck in his hair—thrush feathers, chestnut burrs, thorns of butcher's broom and cabbage rose, worms sucking his spent brains, mushrooms, mosses, galls, sepals), Roland descended into the chaotic heart of things, the center of the square of the cards and of the world, the point of intersection of all possible orders.

His reason? The *Three of Cups* reminded us that it was in a phial kept in the Valley of Lost Reasons, but since the card displayed an overturned cup between two erect cups, it was probable that it was not even preserved in that vessel.

The last two cards in the row were there on the table. The first was *Justice*, which we had met before, surmounted by the frieze of the galloping warrior—a sign that the knights of Charlemagne's Army were following their champion's trail, keeping watch over him, not abandoning the hope of bringing his sword back to the service of Reason and Justice. Was that blond dispenser of justice with her sword and scales the image of Reason, with whom in any event he would finally have to settle his accounts? Was she the Reason of the story,

lurking under the combining Chance of the scattered tarots? Did this mean that, however he may wander, the moment comes when they catch him, Roland, and bind him, and force down his throat the intellect he has rejected?

In the last card we contemplate the paladin strung up by his feet as *The Hanged Man.* And finally his face has become serene and radiant, his eye clearer than ever it was in the exercise of his past reasons. What does he say? He says: "Leave me like this. I have come full circle and I understand. The world must be read backward. All is clear."

The Tale of Astolpho on the Moon

On the subject of Roland's sanity, I would have liked to collect further testimony, especially from the one who had made his recovery a duty, a test for his own ingenious daring. I would have liked him, Astolpho, to be there with us. Among the guests who still had told nothing there was a little fellow, light as a jockey or an elf, who jumped up from time to time, wriggling and trilling as if his muteness and ours were an unparalleled source of amusement for him. Observing him, I realized he might very well be that English knight, and I explicitly urged him to tell us his story, handing him the figure from the pack I thought most resembled him: the gay, rearing *Knight of Clubs*. Our little smiling companion held out a hand, but instead of taking the card he sent it flying, with a flick of his index finger against his thumb. It fluttered like a leaf in the wind and came to rest on the table, toward the base of the square.

Now there were no more windows open in the center of the mosaic; and few cards were still left out of the game.

The English knight picked up an *Ace of Swords* (I recognized Roland's Durendal, idle, hanging from a tree . . .), he moved it toward *The Emperor* (depicted

with the white beard and the ripe wisdom of the en-throned Charlemagne . . .), as if preparing to climb up a vertical column with his story: *Ace of Swords, Emperor, Nine of Cups.* . . . (As Roland's absence from the Frankish Field became prolonged, Astolpho was summoned by King Charles and invited to banquet with him. . . .) Then came the half-naked, half-tattered *Fool* with the feathers on his head, and *Love*, winged god who from his twisted pedestal flings his darts at lovers. ("You surely know, Astolpho, that the prince of our paladins, our nephew Roland, has lost that illumination that distinguishes man and wise beasts from other beasts and madmen, and now in his folly he runs through the woods, decked with birds' feathers, and answers only the chirping of those creatures as if he understood no other language. It would be less grave if he had been reduced to this state by a misguided zeal for Christian penance, for self-humiliation, mortification of the flesh, and punishment of the pride of the mind, because in that case the harm might somehow be compensated by a spiritual benefit, or at least it would be a fact that, if we could not boast of it, we could at least mention without shame, perhaps shaking our head a bit; but the trouble is that he was driven to madness by Eros, the pagan god who, the more he is suppressed, the more devastation he causes. . . .")

The column continued with *The World*, where a fortified city is seen, with a circle around it—Paris in the circle of its ramparts, besieged for months by the Saracens—and with *The Tower*, which depicts with verisimilitude the hurtling of corpses down from the bastions amid torrents of boiling oil and siege machines at work;

and so it described the military situation (perhaps with Charlemagne's very words: "The enemy is pressing at the foot of the heights of Mont Martire and Mont Parnasse, opening breaches at Menilmontant and at Montreuil, setting fires at Porte Dauphine and Porte des Lilas . . .") with only a last card wanting, the *Nine of Swords*, to conclude on a note of hope (just as the Emperor's speech could have no conclusion but this: "Only our nephew could lead us in a sally that would cut through the circle of iron and fire. . . . Go, Astolpho, trace Roland's reason, wherever it may be lost, and bring it back. It is our only salvation! Hasten! Fly!").

What was Astolpho to do? He had a good card up his sleeve: the Arcanum known as *The Hermit*, represented here as an old hunchback with an hourglass in his hand, a soothsayer who overturns irreversible time and sees the After before the Before. So it is to this sage or wizard Merlin that Astolpho turns to discover where Roland's reason is. The hermit reads the trickle of the grains of sand in the hourglass, and so we prepared to read the second column of the story, which was just to the left, from top to bottom: *The Last Judgment, Ten of Cups, The Chariot, The Moon.* . . .

"You must ascend to Heaven, Astolpho" (the angelic Arcanum of *The Last Judgment* indicated a superhuman ascension) "up to the pale fields of the Moon, where an endless storeroom preserves in phials placed in rows" (as in the *Cups* card) "the stories that men do not live, the thoughts that knock once at the threshold of awareness and vanish forever, the particles of the possible discarded in the game of combinations, the solutions that could be reached but are never reached. . . ."

To go up to the Moon (as the Arcanum *The Chariot* offered us a superfluous but poetical reminder), it is the custom to resort to hybrid races of winged horses, a Pegasus, a Hippogryph; the Fairies rear them in their golden stables to yoke them, in twos or threes, to racing chariots. Astolpho had his Hippogryph, so he climbed into the saddle. He rode off into the heavens. The waxing Moon came toward him. It glided. (In the card, *The Moon* was depicted with greater sweetness than it possesses in the portrayal by rustic actors who in midsummer play the drama of Pyramus and Thisbe, but with equally simple allegorical means. . . .)

Then came *The Wheel of Fortune* at the very moment when we were expecting a more detailed description of the world of the Moon, which would allow us to indulge in the old fancies of an upside-down world, where the ass is king, man is four-legged, the young rule the old, sleepwalkers hold the rudder, citizens spin like squirrels in their cage's wheel, and there are as many other paradoxes as the imagination can disjoin and join.

Astolpho had climbed up to seek Reason in the world of the gratuitous, himself the Knight of the Gratuitous. What wisdom would be drawn for the Earth's guidance from this Moon of the poets' ravings? The knight tried to ask this question of the first inhabitant he met on the Moon: the personage portrayed in the First Arcanum, *The Juggler* or *The Magician*; the name and image are uncertainly defined, but here—from the inkwell he holds in his hand as if he were writing—he can be taken for a poet.

On the white fields of the Moon, Astolpho encounters the poet, intent on interpolating into his warp the rhymes of the octaves, the threads of his plots, his reasons and his unreasons. If he inhabits the very center of the Moon —or is inhabited by it, as by his deepest nucleus—he will tell us whether it is true that the Moon contains the universal rhyme-list of words and things, if it is the world full of sense, the opposite of the senseless Earth.

"No, the Moon is a desert." This was the poet's reply, to judge by the last card put down on the table: the bald circumference of the *Ace of Coins*. "From this arid sphere every discourse and every poem sets forth; and every journey through forests, battles, treasures, banquets, bedchambers, brings us back here, to the center of an empty horizon."

La Torre

Il Diavolo

All the Other Tales

The square is now entirely covered with cards and with
stories. My story is also contained in it, though I can no
longer say which it is, since their simultaneous inter-
weaving has been so close. In fact, the task of deciphering the stories one by one has made me neglect until
now the most salient peculiarity of our way of narrating,
which is that each story runs into another story, and as
one guest is advancing his strip, another, from the other
end, advances in the opposite direction, because the
stories told from left to right or from bottom to top can
also be read from right to left or from top to bottom, and
vice versa, bearing in mind that the same cards, presented in a different order, often change their meaning,
and the same tarot is used at the same time by narrators
who set forth from the four cardinal points.

And so, as Astolpho began to recount his adventure,
one of the most beautiful ladies of the company, introducing herself through the amorous profile of the *Queen
of Coins,* was already placing at his path's destination
The Hermit and the *Nine of Swords,* which she needed,
because that is precisely how her story began, when she
interrogated a soothsayer to learn the outcome of the
war that had kept her for years besieged in a city foreign

to her. *The Last Judgment* and *The Tower* brought her
the news that the gods had long since decreed the fall of
Troy. In fact, that fortified and besieged city (*The
World*), which in Astolpho's story was Paris coveted by
the Moors, was seen as Troy by the lady who had been
the long war's prime cause. So here the banquets, resounding with songs and the strumming of lyres (*Ten of
Cups*), were those the Achaeans prepared on the longed-
for day of the city's storming.

At the same time, however, another *Queen* (the minis-
tering one, *of Cups*) advanced, in a story of her own,
toward the story of Roland, along his same path, beginning with *Force* and *The Hanged Man*. So this queen
contemplated a fierce brigand (thus, at least, he had been
described to her) hanging from an instrument of torture,
under *The Sun*, in the verdict of *Justice*. She took pity
on him, approached, gave him drink (*Three of Cups*),
and realized he was an alert and courteous youth (*Page
of Clubs*).

The Arcana *The Chariot, Love, Moon, Fool* (which
had already been used for Angelica's dream, Roland's
madness, the journey of the Hippogryph) were now dis-
puted between the soothsayer's prophecy to Helen of
Troy—"A woman, a queen or goddess, will enter in a
chariot with the victors, and your Paris will fall in love
with her," which drove Menelaus's beautiful and adulterous wife to flee by moonlight from the besieged city,
concealed in humble dress, accompanied only by the
court fool—and the story recounted simultaneously by
the other queen, of how, having fallen in love with the
prisoner, she set him free that night, urging him to
escape, disguised as a vagabond, and then to wait for

her to join him, on her royal chariot, in the darkness of the woods.

The two stories then went on, each toward its conclusion, Helen reaching Olympus (*The Wheel of Fortune*) and presenting herself at the banquet (*Cups*) of the gods, the other queen waiting in vain in the woods (*Clubs*) for the man she had freed until the first golden light (*Coins*) of morning. And as the first, addressing the supreme Zeus (*The Emperor*), concluded: "Tell the poet (*The Juggler*) who here in Olympus, blind no longer, sits among the Immortals and arranges his verses outside of time in temporal poems that other poets will sing, that only this alms (*Ace of Coins*) do I ask of the will of the Celestials (*Ace of Swords*); let him write this in the poem of my destiny: before Paris can betray her, Helen will give herself to Ulysses in the very belly of the Trojan Horse (*Knight of Clubs*)!," the other queen's fate was no less uncertain, as she heard herself addressed by a splendid woman warrior (*Queen of Swords*) who was coming toward her at the head of an army: "Queen of the night, the man you have set free is mine: prepare to do battle; war with the armies of the day does not end, among the trees of the woods, before dawn!"

At the same time, we had to keep in mind that Paris, or Troy, besieged in the card of *The World*, which was also the celestial city of the grave-robber's story, was now becoming a subterranean city in the story of a fellow who had introduced himself in the sturdy, convivial features of the *King of Clubs*, and who had reached that point after he had armed himself in a magic wood with a truncheon of extraordinary powers and had followed an unknown warrior with black arms who boasted

of his riches (*Clubs, Knight of Swords, Coins*). In a tavern brawl (*Cups*), the mysterious traveling companion had decided to gamble the scepter of the city (*Ace of Clubs*). The fight, with cudgels, turned out in our hero's favor, whereupon the Stranger said to him: "Here you are then, master of the City of Death. You have defeated the Prince of Discontinuity." And taking off his mask, he revealed his true countenance (*Death*), a yellow, noseless skull.

When the City of Death was locked, no one could die any more. A new Age of Gold began: men lavished all on merry-making, crossed swords in harmless brawls, flung themselves unhurt from high towers (*Coins, Cups, Swords, Tower*). And the graves inhabited by living revelers (*The Last Judgment*) represented the now-useless cemeteries where the pleasure seekers gathered for their orgies, before the terrified gaze of the angels and of God. So a warning was not long in resounding: "Reopen the gates of Death or the world will become a desert bristling with dry sticks, a mountain of cold metal!" And our hero knelt at the feet of the wrathful Pontiff, in an act of obedience (*Four of Clubs, Eight of Clubs, Eight of Coins, The Pope*).

"I was that Pope!" another guest seemed to exclaim, presenting himself in the disguise of the *Knight of Coins* and scornfully throwing down the *Four of Coins*, which perhaps he meant to signify that he had abandoned the pomp of the papal court to carry the final viaticum to men dying on the field of battle. *Death*, followed by the *Ten of Swords*, then represented the expanse of dismembered bodies amid which the aghast Pontiff wandered, at the beginning of a story related in detail by the same cards that had already marked out the love of a warrior and a corpse but now were read by a different code through which the succession *Clubs, Devil, Two of Coins, Swords* suggested that the Pope, tempted to doubt by the sight of the massacre, was heard to ask himself: "Why do you permit this, God? Why do you allow so many of your souls to be lost?" And from the woods, a voice replied: "There are two of us to share the world (*Two of Coins*) and souls! It is not up to Him alone to allow or not allow. He has always to settle scores with me!"

The *Page of Swords* at the end of the strip made it clear that this voice was followed by the apparition of a warrior with a contemptuous manner: "Recognize in me the Prince of Oppositions, and I will make peace reign in the world (*Cups*); I will begin a New Age of Gold!"

"For a long time this sign has reminded us that the Other has been defeated by the One!" the Pope may have said, answering him with the crossed *Two of Clubs*.

Or else that card indicated a crossroads. "The paths are two. Choose," the Enemy said. But in the center of the crossroads the *Queen of Swords* appeared (formerly the sorceress Angelica or beautiful doomed soul or female captain), to declare: "Stop! Your contest has no sense. Know then that I am the Joyous Goddess of Destruction, who governs the world's ceaseless dissolution and restoration. In the general massacre the cards are continuously shuffled, and souls fare no better than bodies, which at least enjoy the repose of the grave. An endless war racks the universe up to the very stars of the firmament and spares not even spirits or atoms. In the gilded dust suspended in the air, when a room's

darkness is penetrated by rays of light, Lucretius contemplated battles of impalpable corpuscles, invasions, assaults, tourneys, whirlwinds . . ." (*Swords, Star, Coins, Swords*).

Surely my own story is also contained in this pattern of cards, my past, present, and future, but I can no longer distinguish it from the others. The forest, the castle, the tarots have brought me to this point, where I have lost my story, confused it in the dust of the tales, become freed of it. What is left me is only the manic determination to complete, to conclude, to make the sums work out. I still have to cover two sides of the quadrangle in the opposite direction, and I advance only out of punctilio, so as not to leave things half-done.

The innkeeper-lord, our host, is not long in telling his tale. We can assume that he is the *Page of Cups* and that an unusual guest (*The Devil*) has turned up at his inn-castle. With certain customers it is a good practice never to offer free drink, but when he was to pay, the guest said: "Host, in your tavern, everything is contaminated, wines and destinies."

"Your Honor is not content with my wine?"

"Quite content! The only one who can appreciate all that is mingled, two-faced, is myself. So I wish to give you much more than *Two Coins!*"

At this point *The Star*, Arcanum Seventeen, no longer represented Psyche, or the bride emerging from the grave, or a star of the firmament, but only the serving-maid who had been sent to collect the bill and came back, her hands glistening with coins never seen before, as she shouted: "If you only knew! That gentleman! What he

did! He emptied one of the *Cups* on the table and a river
of *Coins* flowed from it!"

"What spell is this?" the innkeeper-lord had exclaimed.

The customer was already at the door. "Among your
cups there is now one that looks like the others, but
instead is magic. Use this gift in a way that will please
me; otherwise, as you have known me as a friend, so I
will return to meet you as an enemy!" he said, and
vanished.

After thinking it over at length, the lord of the castle
had decided to disguise himself as a juggler and go to the
capital, to win power by pouring out ringing coins. So
then *The Juggler* (whom we had seen as a Mephistopheles or as a poet) was also the innkeeper-lord who
dreamed of becoming *Emperor* with the shell games of
his *Cups*, and *The Wheel* (no longer Mill of Gold or
Olympus or World of the Moon) represented his intention of overturning the world.

He set forth. But in the woods . . . At this point we
had once more to interpret the Arcanum of *The Popess*
as a High Priestess who celebrated a ritual feast in the
wood and said to the wayfarer: "Return to the Bacchan-
tes the sacred cup that was stolen from us!" And thus the
barefoot maiden, sprinkled with wine, known in the tarots as *Temperance*, was explained, and so was the elaborate working of the goblet-altar which occupied the
position of the *Ace of Cups*.

At the same time, the gigantic woman who served us
wine like an attentive hostess or solicitous chatelaine had
also begun a story of her own with three cards, *Queen of
Clubs, Eight of Swords, Popess*. We were led to see *The

Popess as a convent's Abbess to whom our storyteller, then a tender schoolgirl, had said, to overcome the terror that reigned among the nuns at the approach of the war: "Let me challenge to a duel (*Two of Swords*) the captain of the invaders!"

This pupil, in fact, was a skilled swordswoman—as *Justice* again revealed to us—and at dawn, on the battlefield, her majestic person made such a dazzling appearance (*The Sun*) that the prince challenged to combat (*Knight of Swords*) fell in love with her. The wedding banquet (*Cups*) was celebrated in the palace of the bridegroom's parents (*Empress* and *King of Coins*), whose countenances expressed all their distrust toward that ungainly daughter-in-law. As soon as the bridegroom had to leave again (the moving away of the *Knight of Cups*), his cruel parents paid (*Coins*) an assassin to take the bride into the woods (*Clubs*) and kill her. But then the brute (*Force*) and *The Hanged Man* proved to be the same person, the assassin who attacked our lioness and found himself, a little later, tied, head downward, by that robust feminine fighter.

Having eluded this ambush, the heroine concealed herself in the guise of a hostess or castle maidservant, as we now saw her both in person and in the Arcanum of *Temperance*, pouring out the purest of wines (as the Bacchic motifs of the *Ace of Cups* assured us). And now she is setting a table for two, awaiting her husband's return and peering at every movement of the foliage of this wood, at every card drawn from this pack of tarots, every turn of events in this pattern of tales, until the end of the game is reached. Then her hands scatter the cards, shuffle the deck, and begin all over again.

The Tavern
of Crossed
Destinies

The Tavern

We come out of the darkness, no, we enter; outside there
is darkness, here something can be seen amid the smoke;
the light is smoky, perhaps from candles, but colors can
be seen, yellows, blues, on the white, on the table, colored patches, reds, also greens, with black outlines, drawings on white rectangles scattered over the table. There
are some *clubs*, thick branches, trunks, leaves, as outside,
before, some *swords* slashing at us, among the leaves,
the ambushes in the darkness where we were lost; luckily
we saw a light in the end, a door; there are some gold
coins that shine, some *cups*, this table arrayed with
glasses and plates, bowls of steaming soup, tankards of
wine; we are safe but still half-dead with fright; we can
tell about it, we would have plenty to tell, each would
like to tell the others what happened to him, what he was
forced to see, with his own eyes in the darkness, in the
silence; here now there is noise, how can I make myself
heard, I cannot hear my voice, my voice refuses to emerge
from my throat, I have no voice, I do not hear the others'
voices either; noises are heard, I am not deaf after all, I
hear bowls scraped, flasks uncorked, a clatter of spoons,
chewing, belching; I make gestures to say I have lost the
power of speech, the others are making the same ges-

tures, they are dumb, we have all become mute, in the forest; all of us are around this table, men and women, dressed well or poorly, frightened, indeed frightful to see, all with white hair, young and old; I too look at my reflection in one of these mirrors, these cards, my hair too has turned white in sudden fear.

How can I tell about it now that I have lost my power of speech, words, perhaps also memory, how can I tell what was there outside; and once I have remembered, how can I find the words to say it, and how can I utter those words? We are all trying to explain something to the others with gestures, grimaces, all of us like monkeys. Thank God, there are these cards, here on the table, a deck of tarots, the most ordinary kind, the Marseilles tarots as they are called, also known as Bergamasque, or Neapolitan, or Piedmontese, call them what you wish, if they are not the same, they are very like those in village taverns, in gypsy women's laps, crudely drawn, coarse, but with unexpected details, not really so easy to understand, as if the person who carved these drawings in wood, to print them, had traced them with his clumsy hands from complex models, refined, with who knows what perfectly studied features, and then he went at them with his chisel, haphazardly, not even bothering to understand what he was copying, and afterward he smeared the wooden blocks with ink, and that was that.

We all grab for the cards at once, some of the pictures aligned with other pictures recall to me the story that has brought me here, I try to recognize what happened to me and to show it to the others, who meanwhile are also hunting there among the cards, pointing a finger at one card or another, and nothing fits properly with anything, and we snatch the cards away from one another, and we scatter them over the table.

The Waverer's Tale

One of us turns over a card, picks it up, looks at it as if he were looking at himself in a mirror. True, the *Knight of Cups* really seems to be he. It is not only the face, anxious, wide-eyed, with long hair, now white, falling to his shoulders; the resemblance can be noted also in his hands, which he moves over the table as if he had no idea where to put them. There in the card the right hand holds an outsize cup balanced on the palm, and the left barely touches the reins with the fingertips. This reeling posture is communicated also to the horse: you would say he is unable to plant his hoofs firmly on the plowed earth.

Having found that card, the young man seems to recognize a special meaning in all the other cards that come within his reach, and he begins lining them up on the table, as if he were following a thread from one to the other. As, next to an *Eight of Cups* and a *Ten of Clubs*, he puts down the Arcanum that, according to the locality, they call *Love* or *The Lover* or *The Lovers*, the sadness to be read in his face suggests a heartache that impelled him to rise from an overheated banquet for a breath of air in the forest. Or actually to desert his own

wedding feast, to run off to the woods on the very day of his marriage.

Perhaps there are two women in his life, and he is unable to choose. This is exactly how the drawing portrays him: still blond, between the two rivals, one seizing him by the shoulder and staring at him with a lustful eye, the other rubbing her whole body against him in a languid movement, while he does not know which way to turn. Every time he is about to decide which of the two would be the more suitable bride, he convinces himself he can very well give up the other, and so he is resigned to losing the latter every time he realizes he prefers the former. The only fixed point in this mental vacillation is that he can do without either one, for every choice has an obverse, that is to say a renunciation, and so there is no difference between the act of choosing and the act of renouncing.

Only a journey could release him from this vicious circle: the tarot the young man now puts on the table will surely be *The Chariot:* the two horses draw the stately vehicle along the rough paths through the forest; the reins are slack, for he habitually lets the animals have their way, so when they reach a crossroads he does not have to make the choice. The *Two of Clubs* marks the crossing of two roads; the horses start tugging, one this way, one that; the wheels are drawn to such a divergence they seem perpendicular to the road, a sign that the chariot has stopped. Or else, if it is moving, it might as well remain still, as happens to many people before whom the ramps of the most smooth and speedy roads open, flying on high pylons, over valleys, piercing granite mountains, and they are free to go everywhere, and everywhere is always the same. Thus we saw him printed there in the falsely decisive pose, like the master of his fate, a triumphant vehicle-driver; but he bore always within him his divided soul, like the two masks with divergent gaze that he wore on his cloak.

To decide which road to take he could only rely on chance: the *Page of Coins* depicts the youth as he throws a coin in the air: heads or tails. Perhaps neither; the coin rolls and rolls, then remains erect in a bush, at the foot of an old oak, right in the middle of the two roads. With the *Ace of Clubs* the youth surely wishes to tell us that, unable to decide whether to continue in one direction or the other, he had no course save to get down from the chariot and climb up a gnarled trunk, among the branches which, with their succession of repeated forks, continue to inflict the torment of choice on him.

He hopes at least that after pulling himself up from one branch to another he will be able to see farther, discover where the roads lead; but the foliage beneath him is dense, the ground is soon out of sight, and if he raises his eyes toward the top of the tree he is blinded by *The Sun*, whose piercing rays make the leaves gleam with every color, against the light. However, the meaning of those two children seen in the tarot should also be explained: they must indicate that, looking up, the young man has realized he is no longer alone in the tree; two urchins have preceded him, scrambling up the boughs.

They seem twins: identical, barefoot, golden blond. Perhaps at this point the young man spoke, asked: "What are you two doing here?" Or else: "How far is it to the top?" And the twins replied, indicating with confused gesticulation toward something seen on the

L'IMPÉRATRICE

horizon of the drawing, beneath the sun's rays: the walls of a city.

But where are these walls located, with respect to the tree? The *Ace of Cups* portrays, in fact, a city, with many towers and spires and minarets and domes rising above the walls. And also palm fronds, pheasants' wings, fins of blue moonfish, which certainly jut from the city's gardens, aviaries, aquariums, among which we can imagine the two urchins, chasing each other and vanishing. And this city seems balanced on top of a pyramid, which could also be the top of the great tree; in other words, it would be a city suspended on the highest branches like a bird's nest, with hanging foundations like the aerial roots of certain plants which grow at the top of other plants.

As they lay down the cards, the young man's hands are increasingly slow and uncertain, and we have ample time to follow him with our conjectures, and to ponder silently the questions that must certainly have come into his head as they now come into ours. "What city is this? Is this the City of All? Is this the city where all parts are joined, all choices balanced, where the void between what we expect of life and what we draw is filled?"

But who was there, in the city, whom the youth could question? Let us imagine he has entered through the arched gate in the girdle of the walls, he has stepped into a square with a high stairway at the end, and at the top of this stairway there is seated a personage with royal attributes, an enthroned divinity or crowned angel. (Behind the personage two protuberances can be seen, which could be the back of the throne, but also a pair of wings, awkwardly traced in the drawing.)

"Is this your city?" the youth must have inquired.

"Yours." He could have received no better answer. "Here you will find what you ask."

Taken by surprise like this, how could he express a sensible request? Hot from his climb to that height, he could have said only: "I am thirsty."

And the enthroned angel said: "You need only choose from which well to drink." And he must have pointed to the two identical wells that open in the deserted square.

You have merely to glance at the youth to realize he feels lost once again. The crowned authority now wields a scales and a sword, the attributes of the angel who keeps watch over decisions and balances, from the summit of the constellation of Libra. Are you then admitted even into the City of All only through a choice and a rejection, accepting one side and rejecting the rest? He might as well leave as he came; but, turning, he sees two *Queens* looking down from two balconies, facing each other from opposite sides of the square. And lo! he seems to recognize the two women of his eluded choice. They seem to be there on guard, to prevent his leaving the city, for in fact each is holding an unsheathed sword, one with her right hand, the other—surely for symmetry's sake—with her left. Or else, while there can be no doubts about one queen's sword, the other's could also be a goose-quill pen, or closed compasses, or a flute, or a paper-knife, and then the two women would signify two different ways open to him who still has to find himself: the way of passions, which is always a way of action, aggressive, with abrupt shifts, and the way of wisdom, which demands reflection and learning little by little.

In arranging and pointing to the cards, the youth's hands now hint at vacillation and changes in the order; now the hands are wrung, regretting every tarot already played, which might better have been kept in reserve for another round, now they droop in limp gestures of indifference, to indicate that all tarots and all wells are the same, like the *cups* which are repeated, identical, in the pack, as, in the world of the uniform, objects and destinies are scattered before you, interchangeable and unchanging, and he who believes he makes decisions is deluded.

How to explain that, with his consuming thirst, neither this well nor that would suffice? What he wants is the cistern where the waters of all wells and all rivers are poured and mingled, the sea depicted in the Arcanum known as *The Star* or *The Stars*, where life's aquatic origins are celebrated as the triumph of mixture and of squandered opulence. A naked goddess takes two jugs containing who knows what juices kept cool for the thirsty (all around there are the yellow dunes of a sun-baked desert), and empties them to water the pebbled shore: and at that instant a growth of saxifrage springs up in the midst of the desert, and among the succulent leaves a blackbird sings; life is the waste of material thrown away, the sea's cauldron merely repeats what happens within constellations that for billions of years go on pounding atoms in the mortars of their explosions, obvious here even in the milk-colored sky.

In the way the youth slams these cards on the table we can almost hear him shouting: "It's the sea! It's the sea I want!"

"And you shall have the sea!" The reply of the astral authority could only announce a cataclysm, the rising of the oceans' level toward the abandoned cities, lapping the paws of the wolves that have taken refuge on the heights and howl toward *The Moon* looming over them, while the army of crustaceans advances from the depth of the abysses to reconquer the globe.

A thunderbolt that strikes the top of the tree, breaking every wall and *tower* of the suspended city, illuminates an even more horrifying sight, for which the youth prepares us, uncovering a card with a slow movement and with terrified eyes. Rising to his feet on his throne, the regal interlocutor changes and becomes unrecognizable: at his back it is not an angelic plumage that opens, but two bat-wings that darken the sky, the impassive eyes have become crossed, oblique, and the crown has sprouted horn branches, the cloak falls to reveal a naked, hermaphroditic body, hands and feet prolonged into talons.

"Why, were you not an angel?"

"I am the angel who dwells in the point where lines fork. Whoever retraces the way of divided things encounters me, whoever descends to the bottom of contradictions runs into me, whoever mingles again what was separated feels my membraned wing brush his cheek!"

At his feet the solar twins have reappeared, transformed into two beings whose features are both human and animal, with horns, tail, feathers, paws, scales, linked to the rapacious character by two long threads or umbilical cords, and it is likewise probable that each of them holds on a leash two other, smaller devils that

have remained outside the picture, so that from branch to branch stretches a network of ropes which the wind sways like a great cobweb, amid a flutter of black wings of decreasing size: noctules, owls, hoopoes, moths, hornets, gnats.

The wind, or waves? The lines drawn at the bottom of the card could indicate that the great tide is already engulfing the top of the tree and all vegetation is being dissolved in a swaying of algae and tentacles. This is the answer to the choice of the man who does not choose: now he does indeed have the sea, he plunges into it headlong, swaying among the corals of the depths, *Hanged* by his feet in the sargassoes that hover half-submerged beneath the ocean's opaque surface, and his green seaweed hair brushes the steep ocean beds. (Is this then the very card that Madame Sosostris, famous clairvoyante but not very reliable as to nomenclature, in prophesying the private and general destiny of the distinguished Lloyds employee, described as a drowned Phoenician sailor?)

If the only thing he wished was to escape from individual limitation, from categories, roles, to hear the thunder that rumbles in molecules, the mingling of prime and ultimate substances, this then is the path that opens to him through the Arcanum known as *The World:* Venus dances in the sky, crowned with vegetation, surrounded by incarnations of multiform Zeus; every species and individual and the whole history of the human race are only a random link in a chain of evolutions and mutations.

He has only to conclude the great turn of *The Wheel* in which animal life evolves and in which you can never say this is the top and this is the bottom, or the even longer turn which passes through decay, the descent to the center of the earth in the deposits of the elements, the awaiting of the cataclysms that shuffle the tarot pack and bring the buried strata to the surface, as in the Arcanum of the final earthquake.

The hands' trembling, the prematurely white hair were only faint signs of what our hapless neighbor had undergone: in that same night he had been chopped (*swords*) into his prime elements, he had gone through the craters of volcanoes (*cups*), through all the eras of the earth, he had risked remaining prisoner of the definitive immobility of crystal (*coins*), and had reappeared in life through the painful blossoming of the forest (*clubs*), until he had resumed his own identical human form, in the saddle, the *Knight of Coins*.

But is this really he or is it rather a double whom he saw coming through the forest, the moment he was restored to himself?

"Who are you?"

"I am the man who was to marry the girl you did not choose, who was to take the other road at the crossing, quench his thirst at the other well. By not choosing, you have prevented my choice."

"Where are you going?"

"To an inn different from the one you will come upon."

"Where shall I see you again?"

"Hanging from a gallows different from the one where you will have hanged yourself. Farewell."

The Tale of the Forest's Revenge

The tale's thread is tangled not only because it is difficult to fit one card to another, but also because, for every new card the young man tries to align with the others, ten hands are outstretched to take it from him and insert it in another story each one is constructing, and at a certain point his cards are escaping him in all directions and he has to hold them in place with his hands, his forearms, his elbows, and so he hides them from anyone trying to understand the story he is telling. Luckily, among all those obtrusive hands there is a pair that comes to his aid, helping him keep the cards in line, and since these hands are as big and as heavy as three ordinary hands, and the wrists and arms are proportionately thick, and proportionate also are the strength and determination with which they pound the table, in the end the cards the wavering young man succeeds in keeping together are those remaining under the protection of the unknown huge hands, a protection due not so much to interest in the story of his indecisions as to the chance juxtaposition of some of those cards in which someone has recognized a story that means more to him, namely his own.

Her own. It is a woman, in fact. Because, their dimen-

sions apart, the form of these fingers and hands and wrists and arms is that which distinguishes female fingers, hands, wrists, and arms, those of a plump girl, well shaped; and, in fact, moving up along those limbs, you follow the figure of a gigantic maiden who, until a short time before, was seated amongst us, quite calm; now all of a sudden, overcoming her awe, she has started gesticulating, digging her elbow into people's stomachs, and knocking her neighbors off the bench.

Our eyes move up to her face, which blushes—whether in shyness or wrath—then down again to the face card of the *Queen of Clubs,* who bears a considerable resemblance to her, in her solid, rustic features, framed by a rich growth of white hair, and in her curt attitude. She has pointed out that card with a tap that seems the banging of a fist on the table, and the moaning that comes from her sulky lips seems to say:

"Yes, that is I, all right, and these thick *clubs* are the forest where I was raised by a father who, having given up all hope of anything good from the civilized world, became a *Hermit* in these woods, to keep me far from the bad influences of human society. I developed my *Strength,* playing with boars and wolves, and I learned that the forest, though it lives on the constant clawing and devouring of animals and vegetables, is governed by a law: strength unable to control itself in time, whether of bison or man or condor, creates a desert around it where you kick the bucket and then serve as pasture for ants and flies. . . ."

This law, which ancient hunters knew well, though no one now remembers it any more, can be deciphered in the inexorable but restrained movement with which the beautiful tamer wrenches a lion's jaws open with her fingertips.

Having grown up in intimacy with wild beasts, she has remained wild in the presence of human beings. When she hears a horse's trot and sees a handsome *Knight* riding along the paths in the wood, she peeps at him through the bushes, runs off, frightened, then takes some shortcuts so as not to lose sight of him. Now she finds him again, *Hanged*, his feet bound to a branch by a passing brigand, who empties his pocket to the last penny. The woodland girl does not think twice: she flings herself on the brigand, wielding her club: bones, tendons, joints, cartilege snap like dry twigs. Here we must suppose that she has taken the young man down from the bough and has brought him around, lion-fashion, by licking his face. From a flask she carries over her shoulder, she pours out *Two Cups* of a beverage whose recipe only she knows: something like fermented juniper juice and sour goat's milk. The knight introduces himself: "I am the Crown Prince of the Empire, the only son of His Majesty. You have saved my life. Tell me how I can reward you."

And she says, "Stay a while and play with me," and she hides among the arbutus bushes. That beverage was a powerful aphrodisiac. He chases her. Quickly the narrator would like to place before our eyes the Arcanum *The World*, as a bashful hint—"In this game, my maidenhead was soon lost . . ."—but the drawing shows without reticence how her nakedness was revealed to the young man, transfigured in an amorous

dance, and how at every turn of this dance he discovered a new merit in her: strong as a lioness, proud as an eagle, maternal as a cow, gentle as an angel.

The prince's infatuation is confirmed by the following tarot, *The Lovers,* which also warns us of a tangled situation: the young man proves to be married, and his lawful spouse has no intention of letting him get away from her.

"Legal fetters count for little in the forest: stay here with me and forget the court, its etiquette, and its intrigue." The girl must have made this proposal, or one equally sensible, to him; for she does not consider that princes can have principles.

"Only *The Pope* can release me from my first marriage. You wait here for me. I shall go, deal with the matter, and return at once." And, climbing onto his *Chariot,* he sets off without even looking back, giving her a modest allowance (*Three Coins*).

Abandoned, after a few cycles of *The Stars,* she is seized by labor pains. She drags herself to the shore of a stream. The wild forest animals know well how to give birth unaided, and she has learned from them. She brings into the light of *The Sun* a pair of twins so sturdy they can already stand on their own feet.

"I shall present myself with my children to ask *Justice* of *The Emperor* in person, who will recognize me as the true wife of his heir and the mother of his descendants," and with this intent she sets off for the capital.

On and on she goes, and the forest never ends. She encounters a man who runs off like a *Fool,* pursued by wolves.

"Where do you think you are going, silly girl? No cities, no empire exists any longer! Roads no longer lead from anywhere to anywhere else! Look!"

The yellow and stunted grass and the sand of the desert cover the asphalt and the sidewalks of the city, jackals howl on the dunes, in the palaces abandoned beneath *The Moon* the windows stand open like hollow eye sockets, rats and scorpions spread from basements and cellars.

And yet the city is not dead: the machines, the engines, the turbines continue to hum and vibrate, every *Wheel's* cogs are caught in the cogs of other wheels, trains run on tracks and signals on wires; and no human is there any longer to send or receive, to charge or discharge. The machines, which have long known they could do without men, have finally driven them out; and after a long exile, the wild animals have come back to occupy the territory wrested from the forest: foxes and martens wave their soft tails over the control panels starred with manometers and levers and gauges and diagrams; badgers and dormice luxuriate on batteries and magnetos. Man was necessary; now he is useless. For the world to receive information from the world and enjoy it, now computers and butterflies suffice.

Thus ends the vengeance of the terrestrial forces released in chain explosions of tornadoes and typhoons. Then the birds, already thought extinct, multiply and swarm from the four cardinal points with deafening screeches. When the human race, which has taken refuge in holes underground, tries to emerge again, it sees the sky darkened by a thick blanket of wings. People recognize the day of *Judgment* as it is shown in

the tarots. And that another card's announcement has also come true: the day will come when a feather will knock down the tower of Nimrod.

The Surviving Warrior's Tale

Even if the girl is the sort who knows her own mind, her tale is not necessarily easier to follow than another. For the cards conceal more things than they tell, and as soon as a card says more, other hands immediately try to pull it in their direction, to fit it into a different story. One perhaps begins to tell a tale on his own, with cards that seem to belong solely to him, and all of a sudden the conclusion comes in a rush, overlapping that of other stories in the same catastrophic pictures.

Here, for example, is a man who looks exactly like an officer on active service, and he has begun by recognizing himself in the *Knight of Clubs;* in fact, he has passed the card around for all to see what a handsomely outfitted mount he was riding when he left the barracks that morning and what a well-fitting uniform he was wearing, garnished with shining plates of armor, with a gardenia in the buckle of a greave. His genuine appearance—he seems to say—was that, and if we see him now dented and lamed, it is all due to the frightful adventure he is preparing to narrate.

But if you look carefully at that portrait, you see it also contains elements that correspond to his present appearance: white hair, raving eye, the lance broken,

CAVALIER·D'ÉPÉE

reduced to a stub. Unless it is not a lance stump (especially since he was holding it in his left hand) but a rolled-up sheet of parchment, a message he had been ordered to deliver, perhaps crossing the enemy lines. Let us suppose that he is a staff officer and has been ordered to reach the headquarters of his sovereign or commander, to hand to him a dispatch on which the battle's outcome depends.

The fighting rages; the knight ends up in the midst of the fray; with their swords the opposing armies hack a path, one into the other's midst as in a *Ten of Swords*. There are two recommended ways of fighting in battle: either plunge into the thick of things, pell-mell, or else choose among the enemies one enemy who suits you and give him a good going-over. Our staff officer sees coming toward him a *Knight of Swords* distinguished from the others by the elegance of his personal and equine equipment: his armor, unlike the others seen around, pieced together with oddments, is complete down to the most trifling detail and is all one color from helmet to greaves: a periwinkle blue, against which the gilded breastplate and shin guards stand out. On his feet he wears slippers of red damask like the horse's saddlecloth. His face, though masked with sweat and dust, shows fine features. He holds his great sword in his left hand, a detail not to be overlooked: left-handed adversaries are to be feared. But our narrator also holds his club in his left hand, so both are left-handed and both are to be feared, opponents worthy of each other.

The *Two Swords*, entwined amid a tumult of twigs, acorns, little leaves, budding flowers, indicate that the pair has gone off to one side for single combat, and with downward slashes and wide swings of their swords, they have pruned the surrounding vegetation. At first it seems to our hero that the periwinkle knight's arm is faster than it is strong, and he has only to plunge at him headlong to overpower him, but the latter rains blows on him with the flat of his sword, enough to drive him into the earth like a nail. The horses are already kicking the air, turned on their backs like tortoises on the ground sown with swords that are twisted like snakes, and still the periwinkle warrior persists, wily as a snake, carapaced as a tortoise. The more furious the duel waxes, the greater the display of virtuosity, the pleasure of discovering in oneself or in the enemy new, unexpected resources: and thus into the constant pounding a dance's grace is gradually introduced.

As he duels, our hero has already forgotten his mission, when high over the forest a trumpet sounds resembling that of the Angel of Judgment in the Arcanum known as *The Judgment* and also as *The Angel:* it is the oliphant that calls the faithful followers of *The Emperor* together. Certainly a grave danger threatens the imperial army: with no further delay the officer must hasten to his sovereign's support. But how can he break off a duel that so engages his honor and his pleasure? He must bring it to an end as quickly as possible, and he starts to regain the distance he moved from his enemy at the trumpet's blast. But where is he, the periwinkle knight? That moment of bewilderment was enough for the adversary to disappear. The officer charges into the woods to follow the alarm summons and at the same time to pursue the fugitive.

He forces his way through the thicket, among clubs

and dried brush and stakes. From card to card, the tale advances in brusque leaps which have somehow to be graduated. The wood ends suddenly. The open country stretches out all around, silent; it seems deserted in the evening's shadow. On closer inspection, you can see that it is crammed with men, a disorderly throng that covers it, leaving no corner clear. But it is a flattened crowd, as if smeared over the surface of the ground: none of these men are standing, they lie on their bellies or on their backs, unable to raise their heads higher than the trampled blades of grass.

Some, which *Death* has not stiffened, are groping as if learning to swim in the mire black with their blood. Here and there a hand burgeons, it opens and closes, as if seeking the wrist from which it was severed, a foot tries to take some light steps no longer with a body to support above the ankles, heads of pages and sovereigns shake their long locks flowing over their eyes, or try to straighten the crooked crown on the white hair and succeed only in digging their chins into the dust and chewing gravel.

"What ruination has fallen upon the imperial army?" This is probably the question the knight asked the first living being he encountered: someone so filthy and tattered that from the distance he resembled the *Fool* tarot, while, seen closer, he has proved to be a wounded, limping soldier, fleeing from the field of slaughter.

In our officer's mute tale the voice of this survivor sounds discordant, hoarse, mumbling in a dialect hard to understand some broken phrases like: "Don't ask dumb questions, Lieutenant! If you've got legs, run! The shoe's on the other foot! That army came from God knows where. Never saw them before, wild devils that they are! Headlong, here they fell on us out of nowhere, and we were soon food for the flies! Protect yourself, Lieutenant, and clear out!" And the wretched soldier is already moving off, showing his private parts through his torn trousers, sniffed by stray dogs as their brother in stink, dragging after him the bundle of loot collected from the corpses' pockets.

It takes more to dissuade our knight from going forward. Sidestepping the jackals' howl, he searches the edges of the field of death. In the light of *The Moon* he sees a gilded shield and a silver *Sword* glisten, hanging from a tree. He recognizes his enemy's arms.

From the next card a spurt of water is felt. A stream flows there below, among the reeds. The unknown warrior is standing on the shore and is taking off his armor. Our officer surely cannot attack him at that moment: he hides, to wait till the other is again armed and able to defend himself.

From the plates of the armor white, tender limbs emerge, from the helmet a cascade of dark hair falls along the back to the point where it curves. That warrior has the skin of a maiden, the flesh of a lady, the bosom and womb of a queen: it is a woman who beneath *The Stars* is crouched over the stream, performing her evening ablutions.

As each new card placed on the table explains or corrects the meaning of the preceding cards, so this discovery confounds the knight's passions and intentions: if, before, his emulation, envy, and chivalrous respect for his brave enemy conflicted with his urgency to win, avenge, overwhelm, now the shame of having been held

at bay by a maiden's arm, the haste to re-establish his outraged supremacy as a male, clash with the longing to declare himself vanquished at once, captured by that arm, by that armpit, by that breast.

The first of these new impulses is the stronger: if the roles of man and woman are shuffled, then the cards must immediately be dealt again, the order tampered with must be restored, for outside it a man no longer knows who he is or what is expected of him. That sword is not a woman's attribute, it is a usurpation. The knight would never take advantage of an adversary of his own sex, surprising him unarmed, and still less would he steal from him secretly, but now he crawls among the bushes, approaches the hanging weapons, grasps the sword with a furtive hand, takes it from the tree, and runs off. "War between man and woman has no rules, no loyalty," he thinks, and he does not yet know, to his misfortune, how right he is.

He is about to disappear into the woods when he feels himself seized by the arms and legs, bound, *Hanged* head down. From every clump of bushes on the shore, naked bathing girls have sprung forth, with long legs, like the girl who rushes forward in the card of *The World* through a gap in the boughs. They are a regiment of gigantic women warriors who have swarmed along the water to refresh themselves after the battle, and to regain their *Strength*, which is like the swift lioness's. In a second they are all upon him, seizing him, flinging him down, tearing him from one another, pinching him, pulling him this way and that, probing him with fingers, tongues, nails, teeth, no, not like that, you girls are mad, leave me alone, what are you doing to me now, not there, stop, you'll ruin me, ouch, ouch, have mercy.

Left there for dead, he is succored by a *Hermit* who, in the light of his lantern, roams over the scenes of the battle, composing the remains of the dead and medicating the wounds of the mutilated. The holy man's words can be surmised from the last cards the narrator places on the table, with trembling hand: "I do not know if it was better for you to survive, O soldier. Defeat and slaughter do not befall only the armies of your flag: the host of the avenging Amazons sweeps away and massacres regiments and empires, spreads over the continents of the globe, for ten thousand years subject to masculine dominion, however fragile. The precarious armistice which kept man and woman confronting each other within the family has broken down: wives, sisters, daughters, mothers no longer recognize us as fathers, brothers, sons, husbands, but only as enemies, and all hasten, weapons in hand, to swell the army of the avengers. The proud strongholds of our sex collapse one by one; no man is spared; those whom they do not kill, they castrate; only a few, chosen as drones for the hive, are granted a reprieve, but they can expect even more atrocious tortures to quell any desire of boasting. For the man who thought he was Man there is no salvation. Vindictive queens will rule for the next millennia."

The Tale of the Vampires' Kingdom

Only one among us does not appear frightened even by the most dire cards; indeed he seems to enjoy a curt familiarity with Arcanum Thirteen. And since he is a burly man much like the one seen in the *Page of Clubs,* and in arranging the cards in line he seems to be toiling at his everyday job, mindful of the regularity of the expanse of rectangles separated by narrow paths, it is natural to think that the piece of wood on which he is leaning in the picture is the handle of a spade sunk into the earth and that he is a gravedigger by profession.

In the uncertain light the cards describe a nocturnal landscape, the *Cups* are arrayed like urns, caskets, graves among the nettles, the *Swords* have a metallic echo like shovels or spades against the leaden lids, the *Clubs* are black like crooked crosses, the gold *Coins* glitter like will-o'-the-wisps. As soon as a cloud discloses the *Moon,* a howling of jackals rises as they scratch furiously at the edges of the graves and fight with scorpions and tarantulas over their putrid feast.

In this nocturnal setting we can imagine a King who advances, puzzled, accompanied by his jester or court dwarf (we have the cards of the *King of Swords* and the *Fool,* which fill the bill perfectly), and we can guess a

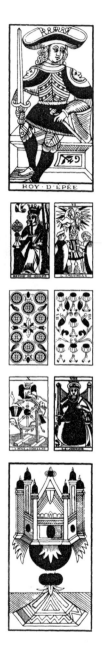

dialogue between them, which the gravedigger overhears. What is the King looking for at this hour? The card of the *Queen of Cups* suggests he is on his wife's trail; the jester has seen her leave the palace stealthily, and, half-joking, half in earnest, he has convinced the sovereign to follow her. Mischief-maker that he is, the dwarf suspects a *Love* intrigue; but the King is sure that anything his wife does can bear the light of the *Sun:* it is her charity work with abandoned children that keeps her constantly on the go.

The King is an optimist by vocation: in his realm everything proceeds for the best, *Coins* circulate and are well invested, *Cups* of abundance are offered to the festive thirst of a prodigal custom, the *Wheel* of the great mechanism turns by its own power day and night, and there is a *Justice* stern and rational like that seen in its card with the set expression of a clerk behind her window. The city he has constructed is many-faceted like a crystal, or like the *Ace of Cups,* pierced by the cheese grater of the skyscrapers' windows, the pulleys of the elevators, auto-coronated by the superhighways, with lots of parking space, burrowed by the luminous anthill of the underground lines, a city whose spires dominate the clouds and whose miasmas' dark wings are buried in the bowels of the earth so as not to dull the view of the great panes of glass and the chromed metals.

The jester, on the other hand, every time he opens his mouth, between a gibe and a prank, sows doubts, denigrating rumors, anxieties, alarms: for him the great mechanism is driven by infernal beasts, and the black wings that sprout beneath the cup-city suggest a snare that threatens it from within. The King has to play along:

does he not give the Fool a salary, deliberately to have himself contradicted and teased? It is an ancient and wise custom at courts for the Fool or Jester or Poet to perform his task of upsetting and deriding the values on which the sovereign bases his own rule, to show him that every straight line conceals a crooked obverse, every finished product a jumble of ill-fitting parts, every logical discourse a blah-blah-blah. And yet from time to time these cranks, wiles, quips, jests arouse a vague uneasiness in the King: this too is surely foreseen, actually guaranteed in the contract between King and Jester, and yet it is a little disturbing all the same, and not only because the only way to make the most of an uneasiness is to be uneasy, but precisely because the King really does become ill at ease.

Like now, when the Fool has led the King into the forest where all of us were lost. "I had no idea forests this thick were still left in my kingdom," the monarch must have remarked, "and at this point, with the things they are saying against me, how I prevent the leaves from breathing oxygen through their pores and digesting light in their green sap, I can only rejoice."

And the Fool says: "If I were Your Majesty, I should not rejoice too much. It is not outside the illuminated metropolis that the forest spreads its shadows, but within: in the heads of your subjects, consequential and executive."

"Are you insinuating that something escapes my control, Fool?"

"That is what we shall see."

The forest's thickness is lessening, with room for paths of turned earth, rectangular pits, a whiteness as of

LA PAPESSE

mushrooms peeping from the ground. With horror we see from the thirteenth tarot that the underbrush is fertilized with half-withered corpses and fleshless bones.

"Why, where have you brought me, Fool? This is a cemetery!"

And the Fool says, pointing to the invertebrate fauna feeding in the graves: "Here a monarch reigns, mightier than you: His Majesty the Worm!"

"I have never seen in my territory a place where the order leaves so much to be desired. What idiot is on duty here?"

"I am, Your Majesty, at your service." And this is the moment when the gravedigger makes his entrance and begins his speech. "To suppress the thought of death the citizens hide the corpses down here, helter-skelter. But then, suppress as they will, they think about it again, and they come back to see if the corpses are sufficiently buried, if the dead, being dead, are really something different from the living, because otherwise the living would not be so sure they are alive, am I right? And so, what with burials and exhumations, digging and covering and stirring around, I'm kept busy." And the gravedigger spits on his hands and starts using his spade again.

Our attention shifts to another card, which seems to want to remain unobtrusive, *The Popess*, and we indicate it to our neighbor with an interrogative gesture which could correspond to a question asked the gravedigger by the King, who has glimpsed a figure hooded in a nun's mantle, crouching among the graves. "Who is that old woman rummaging in the cemetery?"

"God save us! At night a nasty tribe of women roams about here," the gravedigger must have answered, making the sign of the cross, "experts in philters and books of spells, seeking the ingredients for their witchcraft."

"Let us follow her and observe her behavior."

"Not I, Your Majesty!" At this point, the Jester must have drawn back with a shudder. "And I beseech you, give her a wide berth!"

"I must find out, nevertheless, to what extent decrepit superstitions are preserved in my kingdom." You can swear by the King's stubborn character: the gravedigger leads, and he follows.

In the Arcanum called *The Star* we see the woman take off her cloak and her nun's veil. She is not old at all; she is beautiful; she is naked. The moonlight flickers with starry glints and reveals that the cemetery's nocturnal visitor resembles the Queen. First it is the King who recognizes his wife's body, the delicate pear-shaped breasts, the soft shoulders, the generous thighs, the broad and oblong abdomen; then as soon as she raises her brow and shows her face, framed by the heavy hair loose over her shoulders, we too gape: if it were not for her ecstatic expression, which is surely not that of the official portraits, she would be absolutely identical with the Queen.

"How do these foul sorceresses dare assume the appearance of well-bred and exalted people?" This, and no other, must be the reaction of the King, who, in order to dispel any suspicion of his wife, is ready to grant witches a certain number of supernatural powers, including that of transforming themselves at will. He must have promptly rejected an alternative explanation which would better fulfill the demands of verisimilitude ("My wife, poor thing, in her nervous condition, now is afflicted

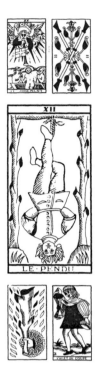

also with sleepwalking!"), seeing the laborious tasks to which the presumed somnambulist devotes herself: kneeling at the edge of a pit, she anoints the earth with murky philters (unless the implements she holds in her hand are to be interpreted actually as acetylene torches scattering sparks, to melt the lead seals of a coffin).

Whatever the operation being performed, here it is a question of a grave being opened, a scene that another tarot foresees for the day of *Judgment* at the end of time, and which instead is being anticipated by the hand of a frail lady. With the help of *Two Clubs* and a rope, the witch extracts from the pit a body *Hanged* by the feet. It is a man's, apparently well preserved; thick almost blue-black hair falls from the pale skull; the eyes are wide as if in violent death; the lips are clenched over the long and sharp canine teeth, which the sorceress bares with a caressing gesture.

In the midst of such horror a detail does not escape us: just as the witch is a double of the Queen, so the corpse and the King are as like as two drops of water. The only one not to notice it is the King himself, who utters a compromising exclamation: "Witch . . . vampire . . . and adulteress!" Does he then admit that the witch and his wife are the same person? Or does he perhaps think that, assuming the Queen's appearance, the witch must also respect her obligations? Perhaps the knowledge of being betrayed with his own Doppel-gänger could console him, but no one has the nerve to tell him.

At the bottom of the grave something indecent is going on: the witch has bent over the corpse like a brooding hen; now the dead man becomes erect as the *Ace of*

Clubs; like the *Page of Cups* he lifts to his lips a goblet the witch has offered him; as in the *Two of Cups* they drink a toast, raising glasses reddish with fresh, unclotted blood.

"My metallic and aseptic kingdom is then still the pasture of vampires, that foul and feudal sect!" The King's cry must be along this line, while his hair, in clumps, stands up on his head, then falls back in place, turned white. The metropolis which he has always believed compact and transparent as a cup carved from rock crystal proves porous and gangrenous like an old cork stuck there, haphazardly, to plug the breach in the damp and infected boundary of the kingdom of the dead.

"I must tell you"—and this explanation can come only from the gravedigger—"on nights of the solstice and the equinox, that sorceress goes to the grave of her husband, whom she herself killed, she digs him up, restores life to him, nourishing him from her own veins, and copulates with him in the great sabbath of bodies that feed their worn arteries on others' blood and warm their perverse and polymorphous pudenda."

The tarots depict two versions of this evil rite, so disparate they might seem the work of two different hands: one, crude, strains to represent an execrable figure, at once man, woman, and bat, named *The Devil;* the other, all festoons and garlands, celebrates the reconciliation of terrestrial forces with those of Heaven, symbolizing the totality of *The World* through the dance of a sorceress or nymph, naked and rejoicing. (But the engraver of the two tarots could be the same individual, a clandestine adept of a nocturnal cult, who sketched with rough lines the bogey of the Devil to mock the

ignorance of exorcists and inquisitors, and lavished his ornamental skills on the allegory of his secret faith.)

"Tell me, my good fellow, how can I free my lands from this scourge?" the King must have asked, and, immediately seized once more by a bellicose impulse (the *swords'* cards are always ready to remind him that the superior strength is on his side), he may have suggested: "I could easily bring out my army, trained in the strategy of encirclement and pressure, in mercilessly using sword and fire, razing to the ground, leaving not a blade of grass, a moving leaf, a living soul. . . ."

"Your Majesty, that would be a mistake," the gravedigger interrupts him; in his nights at the cemetery he must have seen all sorts of unimaginable things. "When the sabbath is caught by the first ray of the rising sun, all the witches and the vampires, incubi and succubi, take flight, some transforming themselves into noctules, some into other bats, some into still other species of Chiroptera. In these guises, as I have had occasion to remark, they lose their usual invulnerability. At that moment, with this hidden trap, we shall capture the sorceress."

"I have faith in what you say, my good man. To work, then!"

Everything goes according to the gravedigger's plan: at least this is what we surmise from the way the King's hand rests on the mysterious Arcanum of *The Wheel*, which can designate the entire whirl of zoomorphous specters, or the trap set up with makeshift materials (the sorceress has fallen into it under the form of a repulsive crowned bat, along with two lemurs, her succubi, spinning in the vortex with no avenue of escape), just as it can also signify the launching ramp where the King has encapsulated his infernal prey to hurl it into an orbit with no return, to expel it from the field of Earth's gravity where everything you throw into the air falls back on your head, perhaps to unload it on the no man's lands of *The Moon*, which has too long governed the whims of werewolves, the generations of mosquitoes, menstruations, and yet claims to remain uncontaminated, clean, pure. The narrator contemplates with anxious gaze the curve that binds the *Two of Coins* as if he were examining the Earth-Moon trajectory, the only way that occurs to him for a radical expulsion of the incongruous from his horizon, provided that Selene, fallen from the pomp of goddess, will resign herself to the rank of celestial garbage can.

A jolt. The night is rent by a flash of lightning, high over the forest, toward the luminous city which at that instant vanishes in the darkness, as if the thunderbolt had fallen on the royal castle, beheading the highest *Tower* that scrapes the sky of the metropolis, or a sudden change of tension in the overloaded circuits of the Great Power Plant had darkened the world in the blackout.

"Short circuit, long night," a proverb of ill augury returns to the mind of the gravedigger and to all of us, imagining ourselves (like Arcanum One, known as *The Juggler*) the engineers who at that moment are desperately dismantling the great Mechanical Brain to discover the fault in the confusion of springs, spools, electrodes, odds and ends.

The same cards in this tale are read and reread with different meanings; the narrator's hand shakes convulsively and points again to *The Tower* and *The Hanged Man* as if inviting us to recognize in an evening news-

paper's blurred telephotos the shots of an atrocious news item: a woman who falls from a dizzying height into the void along the skyscrapers' façades. In the first of these two pictures the fall is well rendered in the groping hands, the reversed skirt, the simultaneity of the double spinning image; the second, a close-up on the body that, before being crushed on the ground, is caught by the feet in some wires, explains the reason of the power failure.

And so we are able to reconstruct mentally the awful event with the breathless voice of the Fool, who overtakes the King: "The Queen! The Queen! She was falling headlong! Glowing! You know what a meteor looks like? She is about to open her wings! No! her paws are bound! Down! Head first! She is caught in the wires and is hanging there! At the height of the high tension! She thrashes, crackles, slams! She kicks the bucket! The royal membrane of our beloved Queen! She swings there, croaked. . . ."

A tumult rises. "The Queen is dead! Our beloved Sovereign! She jumped from the balcony! The King killed her! We must avenge her!" People hasten from all sides, on foot and on horseback, armed with *swords*, *clubs*, *shields*, and they set out *cups* of poisoned blood as bait. "The vampires did it! The kingdom is in the grip of the vampires! The King is a vampire! We must capture him!"

Two Tales of Seeking and Losing

The tavern's customers jostle one another around the table, which has become covered with cards, as they labor to extract their stories from the melee of the tarots, and the more the stories become confused and disjointed, the more the scattered cards find their place in an orderly mosaic. Is this pattern only the result of chance, or is one of us patiently putting it together?

There is an elderly man, for example, who maintains his meditative calm in the midst of the turmoil, and each time, before putting down a card, he studies it as if absorbed in an operation whose successful outcome is not certain, a combination of trivial elements from which, however, a surprising result may emerge. The trim professorial white beard, the grave gaze in which there is a hint of uneasiness, are some of the features he shares with the picture of the *King of Coins*. This portrait of himself, along with the cards of *Cups* and gold *Coins* seen around him, could define him as an alchemist, who has spent his life investigating the combinations of the elements and their metamorphoses. In the alembics and phials he is being handed by the *Page of Cups*, his famulus or assistant, he examines the bubbling of liquids thick as urine, colored by reagents in clouds of indigo or cin-

CAVALIER·D'EPEE

nabar, from which the molecules of the king of metals are to be detached. But the expectation is vain; what remains in the bottom of the vessels is only lead.

It is known to all, or at least it should be, that if the alchemist seeks the secret of gold out of desire for riches his experiments fail: he must instead free himself of all egoism, all personal limitations, become one with the powers that move in the heart of things, and the first real transformation, which is of himself, will be duly followed by others. Having devoted his best years to this Great Work, our elderly neighbor, now that he finds a deck of tarots in his hand, wants to compose again an equivalent of the Great Work, arranging the cards in a square in which, from top to bottom, from left to right, and vice versa, all stories can be read, his own included. But when he seems to have succeeded in deploying the stories of the others, he realizes his own story has been lost.

He is not the only one who seeks in the succession of the cards the path of a change within himself that can be transmitted externally. There is also another, who, with the beautiful heedlessness of youth, feels he recognizes himself in the boldest warrior figure of the whole deck, the *Knight of Swords,* and he confronts the most cutting of *Swords* cards and the sharpest of *Clubs* to reach his goal. But he has to take a roundabout route (as the serpentine sign of the *Two of Coins* indicates), defying (*Two of Swords*) the infernal powers (*The Devil*) called up by Merlin the Magician (*The Juggler*) in the forest of Broceliande (*Seven of Clubs*), if he wants finally to be allowed to sit at the Round Table (*Ten of*

Cups) of King Arthur (*King of Swords*) in the place no knight so far has been worthy of occupying.

If you look carefully, the destination for both the alchemist and the knight-errant should be the *Ace of Cups* which, for the one, contains phlogiston or the philosopher's stone or the elixir of long life, and for the other the talisman guarded by the Fisher King, the mysterious vessel whose first poet lacked time—or else was unwilling—to explain it to us; and thus, since then, rivers of ink have flown in conjectures about the Grail, still contended between the Roman religion and the Celtic. (Perhaps the Champagne troubadour wanted precisely this: to keep alive the battle between *The Pope* and the Druid-*Hermit*. There is no better place to keep a secret than in an unfinished novel.)

So then the problem that these two companions of ours wanted to solve, arranging the cards around the *Ace of Cups*, was at once the Great Work of Alchemy and the Quest for the Grail. In the same cards, one after the other, both can recognize the stages of their Art or Adventure: in *The Sun*, the star of gold or the innocence of the warrior youth; in *The Wheel*, perpetual motion or the spell of the forest; in *Judgment*, death and resurrection (of metals and of the soul) or the heavenly call.

As things stand, the two stories constantly risk stumbling over each other, if the mechanism is not made quite clear. The alchemist is the man who, to achieve transformations of matter, tries to make his soul become as unchangeable and pure as gold; but there is the instance of a Doctor Faust, who inverts the alchemist's rules, makes the soul an object of exchange, and thus hopes

nature will become incorruptible and it will no longer be necessary to seek gold because all elements will be equally precious: the world is gold, and gold is the world. In the same way a knight-errant is one who submits his actions to an absolute and severe moral law, so that natural law can maintain abundance on earth with absolute freedom; but let us try to imagine a Perceval-Parzival-Parsifal who inverts the rule of the Round Table, knightly virtues in him will be involuntary, they will come forth as a gift of nature, like the colors of butterflies' wings, and while performing his exploits with dazed nonchalance, he will perhaps succeed in subduing nature to his will, in possessing the knowledge of the world like an object, in becoming magician and thaumaturge, in healing the wound of the Fisher King, and in restoring green sap to the wasteland.

The mosaic of cards that we are watching, fixed here, is therefore the Work of the Quest that one would like to conclude without work or search. Doctor Faust has wearied of having the instantaneous metamorphoses of metals depend on the slow transformations that take place within himself, he doubts the wisdom accumulated in the solitary life of a *Hermit*, he is disappointed in the powers of his art as he is in this dawdling over the tarot combinations. At that moment a thunderbolt illuminates his little cell at the top of *The Tower*. A personage appears before him with a broad-brimmed hat, such as the students wear at Wittenberg, a wandering clerk perhaps, or a charlatan *Juggler*, a mountebank at a fair, who has laid out on a stand a laboratory of ill-assorted jars.

"Do you believe you can counterfeit my art?" So the

true alchemist must have addressed the impostor. "What messes are you stirring in your pots?"

"The broth that was at the origin of *The World*," the stranger may have replied, "whence crystals and plants took their form, and the species of animals and the race of Homo Sapiens!" And what he names then appears in the transparent material boiling in an incandescent crucible, just as we now observe it in Arcanum XXI. In this card, which has the highest number of all the tarots and is the one that counts most in players' scoring, a naked goddess framed in myrtle is flying, Venus perhaps; the four figures around her can be recognized as more modern devout emblems, but perhaps they are only a prudent disguise of other apparitions less incompatible with the triumph of the goddess in the middle, perhaps centaurs, sirens, harpies, gorgons, who supported the world before the authority of Olympus had subdued it, or perhaps dinosaurs, mastodons, pterodactyls, mammoths, the attempts nature made before resigning herself—we do not know for how much longer—to human dominion. And there are also those who, in the central figure, see not Venus but the Hermaphrodite, symbol of the souls that reach the center of the world, the culminating point of the itinerary the alchemist must follow.

"And can you then make gold?" the doctor must have asked, to which the other must have replied, "Look!" giving him a brief vision of strongboxes brimming with homemade ingots.

"And can you restore my youth?"

Now the tempter shows him the Arcanum of *Love*, in which the story of Faust is mingled with that of Don

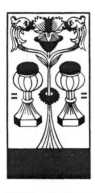

Juan Tenorio, also surely concealed within the network of the tarots.

"What do you want in exchange for the secret?"

The card of the *Two of Cups* is a memorandum of the secret of making gold; and it can be read as the spirits of Sulphur and Mercury which are separated, or as the union of the Sun and the Moon, or the conflict between the Stable and the Volatile, recipes to be found in all the treatises, but to make them work you can spend a whole life blowing on stoves without getting anywhere.

Our neighbor seems to be deciphering in the tarots a story still taking place within himself. But for the moment it does not really look as if we can expect any unforeseen developments: the *Two of Coins* with rapid, graphic efficacy is indicating an exchange, a barter, a do-ut-des; and since the counter-item in this exchange can only be the soul of our companion, it is convenient for us to recognize an ingenuous allegory of it in the fluid, winged apparition of the Arcanum *Temperance;* and if it is traffic in souls that the shady sorcerer is concerned with, there are no doubts about his identity as *The Devil*.

With the help of Mephistopheles, Faust's every wish is promptly satisfied. Or, rather, to tell it straight, Faust receives the equivalent in gold of what he wishes.

"And are you not content?"

"I believed wealth was different, the multiple, the changing, and I see nothing but pieces of uniform metal which come and go and are accumulated, and serve only to multiply themselves, always the same."

Everything his hands touch is transformed into gold. So the story of Doctor Faust mingles also with that of

King Midas, in the card of the *Ace of Coins*, which portrays the terrestrial globe turned into a sphere of solid gold, made arid in its abstraction into money, inedible and unlivable.

"Do you already regret having signed the pact with the Devil?"

"No, the mistake was to barter a single soul for a single metal. Only if Faust compromises himself with many devils at once will he save his plural soul, find wisps of gold at the bottom of plastic matter, see Venus constantly reborn on the shores of Cyprus, dispelling oil slicks, detergent's foam. . . ."

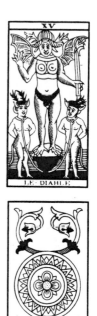

The Arcanum XVII, which can conclude the story of the doctor of alchemy, can also begin the story of the adventurous champion, illustrating his outdoor birth under the stars. Son of an unknown father and of a deposed and fugitive queen, Parsifal bears with him the mystery of his origin. To prevent his knowing more, his mother (who must have had her own good reasons) has taught him never to ask questions, has brought him up in solitude, exempting him from the hard novitiate of chivalry. But knights-errant roam even in those rough moors, and the boy, without asking anything, joins up with them, takes arms, climbs into the saddle, and tramples his overprotective mother beneath his horse's hoofs.

Son of a guilty cohabitation, matricide unawares, soon involved in an equally forbidden love, Parsifal runs lightly through the world, in perfect innocence. Ignorant of everything that must be learned if one is going to get ahead in this world, he behaves according to the rules of

LA·MAISON·DIEV

LA·LUNE

ROY·DE·DENIERS

chivalry because that is how he is made. And radiant with bright ignorance he travels through localities weighed down by a dark awareness.

Wastelands stretch out in the tarot of *The Moon.* On the shore of a lake of dead water there is a castle on whose *Tower* a curse has fallen. Amfortas, the Fisher King, lives there, and we see him here, old and infirm, pressing a wound that refuses to heal. Until that wound is cured, the wheel of transformations will be still, the wheel that passes from the light of the sun to the green of the leaves and to the gaiety of the equinox festivities in spring.

Perhaps the sin of King Amfortas is a cluttered wisdom, a saddened knowledge, kept perhaps at the bottom of the vessel Parsifal sees carried in procession up the steps of the castle, and he would like to know what it is, but still he remains silent. Parsifal's strong point is that he is so new to the world and so occupied with the fact of being in the world that it never occurs to him to ask questions about what he sees. And yet one question of his would suffice, a first question that releases the question of everything in the world that has never asked anything, and then the deposit of centuries collected at the bottom of pots in excavations is dissolved, the eras crushed among the telluric strata begin to flow again, the future recovers the past, the pollen of the abundant seasons buried for millennia in peat bogs starts drifting once more, rising on the dust of the years of drought. . . .

I do not know for how long (hours or years) Faust and Parsifal have been intent on retracing their routes, card after card, on the table of the tavern. But every time they bend over the tarots, their story reads another way, undergoes corrections, variants, affected by the moods of the day and the train of thoughts, oscillating between two poles: all and nothing.

"The world does not exist," Faust concludes when the pendulum reaches the other extreme, "there is not an all, given all at once: there is a finite number of elements whose combinations are multiplied to billions of billions, and only a few of these find a form and a meaning and make their presence felt amid a meaningless, shapeless dust cloud; like the seventy-eight cards of the tarot deck in whose juxtapositions sequences of stories appear and are then immediately undone."

Whereas this would be the (still temporary) conclusion of Parsifal: "The kernel of the world is empty, the beginning of what moves in the universe is the space of nothingness, around absence is constructed what exists, at the bottom of the Grail is the Tao," and he points to the empty rectangle surrounded by the tarots.

STORY OF
HAMLET

STORY OF
OEDIPUS

STORY OF
JUSTINE

STORY OF THE WAVERER

STORY OF THE GIANTESS

STORY OF PARSIFAL

STORY OF THE GRAVEDIGGER

STORY OF THE WARRIOR

STORY OF THE WRITER

STORY OF
KING LEAR

STORY OF
FAUST

STORY OF
LADY MACBETH

I Also Try to Tell My Tale

I open my mouth, I try to articulate words, I grunt, this would be the moment for me to tell my tale, it is obvious that the cards of these other two are also the cards of my story, the story that has brought me here, a series of nasty encounters that is perhaps only a series of missed encounters.

To begin, I have to attract attention to the card called the *King of Clubs*, in which you see a seated person who, if no one else claims him, could very well be me: especially since he is holding an implement with the point downward as I am doing at this moment, and in fact this implement, on closer inspection, resembles a pen or a quill or a well-sharpened pencil or a ballpoint, and if its size seems excessive that must signify the importance this writing implement has in the existence of the above-mentioned sedentary person. As far as I know, the black line that comes from the tip of that cheap scepter is precisely the path that has led me here, and it is therefore not impossible that the *King of Clubs* is the appellative due me, and in that case the term *Clubs* must be understood also in the sense of those vertical lines children learn in penmanship class, the first stammering of those who try to communicate by drawing signs, or in the sense

of the poplar wood from which the white cellulose is pulped and quires of sheets are unrolled, ready to be (and again meanings interlock) penned.

The *Two of Coins* for me too is a sign of exchange, of that exchange that is in every sign, from the first scrawl made in such a way as to be distinguished from the other scrawls of the first writer, the sign of writing wed to exchanges of other things, invented not accidentally by the Phoenicians, involved in the currents of currency as in the circulation of gold coins, the letter that must not be taken literally, the letter that transfers values that without a letter are valueless, the letter always ready to grow upon itself and deck itself with blossoms of the sublime, you see it here illuminated and beflowered on its meaningful surface, the letter as prime element of Belles-Lettres, though always enfolding in its significant coils the currency of significance, the letter Ess that twists to signify it is ready and waiting to signify significations, the signifying sign that has the form of an Ess so that its significations can also assume the form of Ess.

And all those *cups* are nothing but dried-up inkwells waiting for the demons to rise to the surface from the darkness of the ink, the infernal powers, the bogeymen, the hymns to the night, the flowers of evil, the hearts of darkness, or else for the melancholy angel to glide by that distills the humors of the soul and decants states of grace and epiphanies. But no. The *Page of Cups* depicts me as I bend to peer into the envelope of myself; and I do not look content: it is futile to shake and squeeze, the soul is a dry inkwell. What *Devil* would accept it in payment to guarantee me the success of my work?

The Devil should be the card that, in my profession, is

most often encountered: is not the raw material of writing all a rising to the surface of hairy claws, cur-like scratching, goat's goring, repressed violences that grope in the darkness? But the thing can be seen in two ways: this demoniacal teeming inside single and plural persons, in deeds done or thought to have been done, in words said or thought to have been said, can be a way of doing and saying that is wrong, and it is best to press everything down below; or else it may instead be what counts most and since it exists it is advisable to allow it to come out; two ways of seeing the thing which then, in turn, are variously mingled, because it could be, for example, that the negative is negative but necessary because without it the positive is not positive, or else the negative may not be negative at all, and the only negative, if anything, is what we believe positive.

In this case the man who writes can only try to follow an unattainable model: the Marquis so diabolical as to be called divine, who impelled the word to explore the black frontiers of the thinkable. (And the story we should try to read in these tarots will be that of the two sisters who could be the *Queen of Cups* and the *Queen of Swords*, one angelic and the other perverse. In the convent where the former has taken the veil, as soon as she turns around a *Hermit* flings her down and takes advantage of her charms from behind; when she complains, the Abbess, or *Popess*, says: "You do not know the world, Justine: the power of money (*coins*) and of the *sword* chiefly enjoys making objects of other human beings; the varieties of pleasure have no limits, like the combinations of conditioned reflexes; it is all a matter of deciding who is to condition the reflexes. Your sister Juliette can initiate

you into the promiscuous secrets of *Love;* from her you can learn that there are those who enjoy turning the *Wheel* of tortures and those who enjoy being *Hanged* by their feet.")

All this is like a dream which the word bears within itself and which, passing through him who writes, is freed and frees him. In writing, what speaks is what is repressed. And then the white-bearded *Pope* could be the great shepherd of souls and interpreter of dreams Sigismund of Vindobona, and for confirmation, the only thing is to see if somewhere in the rectangle of tarots it is possible to read that story which, according to the teachings of his doctrine, is hidden in the warp of all stories. You take a young man, *Page of Coins,* who wants to drive from himself a dark prophecy: patricide and marriage to his own mother. You send him off at random on a richly adorned *Chariot.* The *Two of Clubs* marks a crossroads on the dusty highway, or, rather, it is the crossroads, and he who has been there can recognize the place where the road that comes from Corinth crosses the one that leads to Thebes. The *Ace of Clubs* reports a street—or, rather, road—brawl, when two chariots refuse to give way and remain with the axles of their wheels locked, and the drivers leap to the ground enraged and dusty, shouting exactly like truckdrivers, insulting each other, calling each other's father and mother pig and cow, and if one draws a knife from his pocket, the consequences are likely to be fatal. In fact, here there is the *Ace of Swords,* there is *The Fool,* there is *Death:* it is the stranger, the one coming from Thebes, who is left on the ground; that will teach him to control his nerves; you, Oedipus, did not do it on purpose, we know that; it was temporary insanity; but meanwhile you had flung yourself on him, armed, as if all your life you had been waiting for nothing else. Among the next cards there is *The Wheel of Fortune*, or Sphinx, there is the entrance into Thebes like a triumphant *Emperor*, there are the *cups* of the feast of the wedding with Queen Jocasta, whom we see here portrayed as the *Queen of Coins*, in widow's weeds, a desirable if mature woman. But the prophecy is fulfilled: the plague infests Thebes, a cloud of germs falls on the city, floods the streets and the houses with miasmas, bodies erupt in red and blue buboes and drop like flies in the streets, lapping the water of the muddy puddles with parched lips. In these cases the only thing to do is consult the Delphic Sibyl, asking her to explain what laws or taboos have been violated: the old woman with the tiara and the open book, tagged with the strange epithet of *Popess*, is she. If you like, in the Arcanum called *Judgment* or *The Angel* you can recognize the primal scene to which the Sigismundian doctrine of dreams harks back: the tender little angel who wakes at night and among the clouds of sleep sees the grownups doing something, he does not know what, all naked and in incomprehensible positions, Mummy and Daddy and other guests. In the dream fate speaks. We can only make note of it. Oedipus, who knew nothing about it, tears out the light of his eyes: literally, the *Hermit* tarot shows him as he takes a light from his eyes, and sets off on the road to Colonus with the pilgrim's cloak and staff.

Of all this, writing warns like the oracle and purifies like the tragedy. So it is nothing to make a problem of. Writing, in short, has a subsoil which belongs to the species, or at least to civilization, or at least to certain

income brackets. And I? And that amount, large or small, of myself, exquisitely personal, that I believed I was putting into it? If I can call up an author's shade to accompany my distrustful steps in the territories of individual destiny, of the ego, of (as they now say) "real life," it should be that of the Egotist of Grenoble, the provincial out to conquer the world, whom I once read as if I were expecting from him the story I was to write (or live: there was a confusion between the two verbs, in him, or in the me of that time). Which of these cards would he point out to me, if he were still to answer my call? The cards of the novel I have not written, with *Love* and all the energy it sets in motion and the fears and the deceits, the triumphal *Chariot* of ambition, the *World* that comes toward you, the happiness promised by beauty? But here I see only the blocks of scenes that are repeated, the same, the routine of the daily grind, beauty as the picture magazines photograph it. Was this the prescription I was expecting from him? (For the novel and for something obscurely related to the novel: "life"?) What is it that kept all this together and has gone away?

Discarding first one tarot, then another, I find myself with few cards in my hand. The *Knight of Swords*, the *Hermit*, the *Juggler* are still me as I have imagined myself from time to time, while I remain seated, driving the pen up and down the page. Along paths of ink the warrior impetuosity of youth gallops away, the existential anxiety, the energy of the adventure spent in a slaughter of erasures and crumpled paper. And in the card that follows I find myself in the dress of an old monk, isolated for years in his cell, a bookworm searching by the lantern's light for a knowledge forgotten among footnotes and index references. Perhaps the moment has come to admit that only tarot number one honestly depicts what I have succeeded in being: a juggler, or conjurer, who arranges on a stand at a fair a certain number of objects and, shifting them, connecting them, interchanging them, achieves a certain number of effects.

The trick of arranging some tarots in a line and making stories emerge from them is something I could perform also with paintings in museums: putting, for example, a Saint Jerome in the place of the *Hermit*, a Saint George in the place of the *Knight of Swords*, to see what comes out. They are, as it happens, the painting subjects that have most attracted me. In museums I always enjoy stopping at the Saint Jeromes. The painters portray the hermit as a scholar consulting treatises outdoors, seated at the mouth of a cave. A little farther on a lion is curled up, domestic, serene. Why the lion? Does the written word tame passions? Or subdue the forces of nature? Or does it find a harmony with the inhumanity of the universe? Or incubate a violence, held back but always ready to spring, to claw? Explain it as you will, painters have been pleased to show Saint Jerome with a lion (taking as genuine the old tale of the thorn in the paw, thanks to the usual mistake of a copyist), and so it gives me satisfaction and security to see them together, to try to recognize myself there, not particularly in the saint or even in the lion (though, for that matter, the two often resemble each other), but in the pair together, in the whole, in the picture, figures, objects, landscape.

In the landscape the objects of reading and writing are

placed among rocks, grass, lizards, having become products and instruments of the mineral-vegetable-animal continuum. Among the hermit's bric-a-brac there is also a skull: the written word always takes into consideration the erasure of the person who has written or the one who will read. Inarticulate nature comprehends in her discourse the discourse of human beings.

But remember we are not in the desert, in the jungle, on Crusoe's island: the city is only a step away. The paintings of hermits, almost always, have a city in the background. An engraving by Dürer is completely occupied by the city, a low pyramid carved with squared towers and peaked roofs; the saint, flattened against a hillock in the foreground, has his back to the city and does not take his eyes off his book, beneath his monk's hood. In Rembrandt's drypoint the high city dominates the lion, who turns his muzzle around, and the saint below, reading blissfully in the shadow of a walnut tree, under a broad-brimmed hat. At evening the hermits see the lights come on at the windows; the wind bears, in gusts, the music of festivities. In a quarter of an hour, if they chose, they could be back among other people. The hermit's strength is measured not by how far away he has gone to live, but by the scant distance he requires to detach himself from the city, without ever losing sight of it.

Or else the solitary writer is shown in his study, where a Saint Jerome, were it not for the lion, could easily be mistaken for a Saint Augustine: the job of writing makes individual lives uniform, one man at a desk resembles every other man at a desk. But in addition to the lion, other animals visit the scholar's solitude, discreet messengers from the outside world: a peacock (Antonello da Messina, London), a wolf cub (another engraving of Dürer's), a Maltese spaniel (Carpaccio, Venice).

In these paintings of interiors, what counts is how a certain number of quite distinct objects are set in a certain space and allow light and time to flow over their surface: bound volumes, parchment scrolls, hourglasses, astrolabes, shells, the sphere hanging from the ceiling which shows how the heavens rotate (in Dürer, its place is taken by a pumpkin). The Saint Jerome–Saint Augustine figure can be seated squarely in the center of the canvas, as in Antonello, but we know that the portrait includes the catalogue of objects, and the space of the room reproduces the space of the mind, the encyclopaedic ideal of the intellect, its order, its categories, its calm.

Or its restlessness: Saint Augustine, in Botticelli (Uffizi), begins to grow nervous, crumples page after page and throws them on the ground beneath the desk. Also in the study where there reigns meditative serenity, concentration, ease (I am still looking at the Carpaccio), a high-tension current passes: the scattered books left open turn their pages on their own, the hanging sphere sways, the light falls obliquely through the window, the dog raises his nose. Within the interior space there hovers the announcement of an earthquake: the harmonious intellectual geometry grazes the borderline of paranoid obsession. Or is it the explosions outside that shake the windows? As only the city gives a meaning to the bleak landscape of the hermit, so the study, with its silence and its order, is simply the place where the oscillations of the seismographs are recorded.

For years now I have been shut up in here, brooding

over a thousand reasons for not putting my nose outside, unable to find one that gives my spirit peace. Do I perhaps regret more extroverted ways of expressing myself? There was also a time when, wandering through museums, I would stop to face and question the Saint Georges and their dragons. The paintings of Saint George have this virtue: you can tell the painter was pleased to have to paint a Saint George. Because Saint George can be painted without believing too much in him, believing only in painting and not in the theme? But Saint George's position is shaky (as a legendary saint, too similar to the Perseus of the myth; as a mythical hero, too similar to the younger brother of the fairy tale), and painters always seem to have been aware of this, so they always looked on him with a somewhat "primitive" eye. But, at the same time, believing: in the way painters and writers have of believing in a story that has gone through many forms, and with painting and repainting, writing and rewriting, if it was not true, has become so.

Even in the painters' pictures, Saint George always has an impersonal face, not unlike the *Knight of Swords* of the cards, and his battle with the dragon is a scene on a coat of arms, fixed outside of time, whether you see him galloping with his lance at rest, as in Carpaccio, charging from his half of the canvas at the dragon who rushes from the other half, and attacking with a concentrated expression, his head down, like a cyclist (around, in the details, there is a calendar of corpses whose stages of decomposition reconstruct the temporal development of the story), or whether horse and dragon are superimposed, monogram-like, as in the Louvre Raphael, where Saint George is using his lance from above, driving it down into the monster's throat, operating with angelic surgery (here the rest of the story is condensed in a broken lance on the ground and a blandly amazed virgin); or in the sequence: princess, dragon, Saint George, the animal (a dinosaur!) is presented as the central element (Paolo Uccello, in London and Paris); or whether Saint George comes between the dragon in the rear and the princess in the foreground (Tintoretto, London).

In any case, Saint George performs his feat before our eyes, always closed in his breastplate, revealing nothing of himself: psychology is no use to the man of action. If anything, we could say psychology is all on the dragon's side, with his angry writhings: the enemy, the monster, the defeated have a pathos that the victorious hero never dreams of possessing (or takes care not to show). It is a short step from this to saying that the dragon is psychology: indeed, he is the psyche, he is the dark background of himself that Saint George confronts, an enemy who has already massacred many youths and maidens, an internal enemy who becomes an object of loathsome alien-ness. Is it the story of an energy projected into the world, or is it the diary of an introversion?

Other paintings depict the next stage (the slaughtered dragon is a stain on the ground, a deflated container), and reconciliation with nature is celebrated, as trees and rocks grow to occupy the whole picture, relegating to a corner the little figures of the warrior and the monster (Altdorfer, Munich; Giorgione, London); or else it is the festivity of regenerated society around the hero and the princess (Pisanello, Verona; and Carpaccio, in the later pictures of the Schiavoni cycle). (Pathetic implicit meaning: the hero being a saint, there will not be a wedding but a baptism.) Saint George leads the dragon on a leash into the square to execute him in a public ceremony. But in all this festivity of the city freed from a nightmare, there is no one who smiles: every face is grave. Trumpets sound and drums roll, we have come to witness capital punishment, Saint George's sword is suspended in the air, we are all holding our breath, on the point of understanding that the dragon is not only the enemy, the outsider, the other, but is us, a part of ourselves that we must judge.

Along the walls of San Giorgio degli Schiavoni, in Venice, the stories of Saint George and Saint Jerome follow one another, as if they were a single story. And perhaps they really are one story, the life of the same man: youth, maturity, old age, and death. I have only to find the thread that links the chivalrous enterprise with the conquest of wisdom. But just now, had I not managed to turn Saint Jerome toward the outside and Saint George toward the inside?

Let us stop and think. If you consider carefully, the element common to both stories is the relationship with a fierce animal, the dragon-enemy or the lion-friend. The dragon menaces the city; the lion, solitude. We can consider them a single animal: the fierce beast we encounter both outside and inside ourselves, in public and in private. There is a guilty way of inhabiting the city: accepting the conditions of the fierce beast, giving him our children to eat. There is a guilty way of inhabiting solitude: believing we are serene because the fierce beast has been made harmless by a thorn in his paw. The hero of the story is he who in the city aims the point of his lance at the dragon's throat, and in solitude keeps the lion with him in all its strength, accepting it as guard and domestic genie, but without hiding from himself its animal nature.

So I have succeeded in coming to a conclusion, I can consider myself satisfied. But will I not have been too pontifical? I reread. Shall I tear it all up? Let us see. The first thing to be said is that the Saint George–Saint Jerome story is not one with a before and an after: we are in the center of a room with figures who present themselves to our view all together. The character in question either succeeds in being warrior and sage in everything he does and thinks, or he will be no one, and the same beast is at once dragon-enemy in the daily massacre of the city and lion-guard in the space of thoughts: and he does not allow himself to be confronted except in the two forms together.

Thus I have set everything to rights. On the page, at least. Inside me, all remains as before.

Three Tales of Madness and Destruction

Now that we have seen these greasy pieces of cardboard become a museum of old masters, a theater of tragedy, a library of poems and novels, the silent brooding over down-to-earth words bound to come up along the way, following the arcane pictures, can attempt to soar higher, to peal forth winged words, perhaps heard in some theater balcony, where their resonance transforms moth-eaten sets on a creaking stage into palaces and battle-fields.

In fact, the three who now started quarreling did so with solemn gestures as if declaiming, and while all three pointed to the same card, with their free hand and with evocative grimaces they exerted themselves to convey that those figures were to be interpreted this way and not that. Now in the card whose name varies according to custom and language—*The Tower, The House of God, The House of the Devil*—a young man carrying a sword, you would say for the purpose of scratching his flowing blond hair (now white), recognizes the platform before Elsinore castle when the night's blackness is rent by an apparition which freezes the sentinels in fear: the majestic march of a ghost whose grizzled beard and shining helmet and breastplate cause him to resemble both the

tarots' *Emperor* and the late king of Denmark, who has returned to demand *Justice*. In such questionable shape, the cards lend themselves to the young man's silent interrogation: "Why the sepulchre hath op'd his ponderous and marble jaws that thou, dead corse, again, in complete steel, revisit'st thus the glimpses of *The Moon?*"

He is interrupted by a lady who, with distraught eye, insists she recognizes in that same *Tower* the castle of Dunsinane when the vengeance darkly prophesied by the witches will be unleashed: Birnam Wood will move, climbing the slopes of the hill, hosts and hosts of trees will advance, their roots torn from the earth, their boughs outstretched as in the *Ten of Clubs*, attacking the fortress, and the usurper will learn that Macduff, born through a sword's slash, is the one who, with a slash of the *Sword*, will cut off his head. And thus the sinister juxtaposition of cards finds a meaning: *Popess*, or prophesying sorceress; *Moon*, or night in which thrice the brinded cat hath mew'd, and the hedgepig whin'd, and newt, frog, and adders allow themselves to be caught for the broth; *Wheel*, or stirring of the bubbling cauldron where witches' mummy is dissolved with gall of goat, wool of bat, finger of birth-strangled babe, poisoned entrails, tails of shitting monkeys, just as the most senseless signs the witches mix in their brew sooner or later find a meaning that confirms them and reduces you, you and your logic, to a gruel.

But an old man's trembling finger is now pointed at the Arcanum of the Tower and the Thunderbolt. In his other hand he holds up the figure of the *King of Cups*, surely to make us recognize him, since no royal attributes remain on his derelict person: nothing in the world has been left him by his unnatural daughters (this is what he seems to say, pointing to two portraits of cruel, crowned ladies and then at the squalid landscape of the *Moon*), and now others want to usurp even this card from him, the proof of how he was driven from his palace, emptied from the walls like a can of rubbish, abandoned to the fury of the elements. Now he inhabits the storm and the rain and the wind as if he could have no other home, as if the world were allowed to contain only hail and thunder and tempest, just as his mind now houses only wind and thunderbolts and madness. Blow, winds, and crack your cheeks! You cataracts and hurricanoes, spout till you have drench'd our steeples, drown'd the cocks! You sulphurous and thought-executing fires, vaunt-couriers to oak-cleaving thunderbolts, singe my white head! And thou, all-shaking thunder, smite flat the thick rotundity o' the world! Crack nature's molds, all chromosomes spill at once that make ungrateful man! We read this hurricane of thoughts in the eyes of the old sovereign seated in our midst, his bent shoulders huddled no longer in his ermine mantle but in a *Hermit*'s habit, as if he were still wandering by lantern light over the heath without shelter, the *Fool* his only support and mirror of his madness.

Instead, for the young man ahead of him the *Fool* is merely the role he has set himself to play, the better to work out a revenge plot and to conceal his spirit, distraught by the revelation of the guilty deeds of his mother, Gertrude, and his uncle. If this is neurosis, there is a method in it, and in every method, neurosis. (We know this well, glued to our game of tarots.) It was the story of relations between the young and the old that he, Hamlet, had come to tell us: the more fragile youth feels

itself in the face of age's authority, the more it is driven to form an extreme and absolute idea of itself, and the more it remains dominated by looming parental phantoms. The young arouse similar uneasiness in the old: they loom like ghosts, they wander around hanging their heads, digging up remorses the old had buried, scorning what the old believe their finest possession: experience. So let Hamlet play the fool, with his stockings ungartered and a book open under his nose: the ages of transition are subject to mental ailments. For that matter, his mother has surprised him (*The Lover!*) raving for Ophelia: the diagnosis is quickly made, we shall call it love-madness and thus all is explained. If anything, Ophelia, poor angel, will be the one who pays: the Arcanum that defines her is *Temperance* and already foretells her watery death.

Here is *The Juggler* to announce that a company of mountebanks or strolling players has arrived to perform at court: it is an opportunity to confront the guilty parties with their misdeeds. The play tells of an adulterous and murdering *Empress:* does Gertrude recognize herself? Claudius runs off, upset. From this moment on, Hamlet knows that his uncle spies on him from behind the curtains: a smart blow of the *Sword* against a moving arras would be enough to fell the king. How now! A rat? Dead, for a ducat, dead! But no: it was not the king hidden there but (as the card called *The Hermit* reveals) old Polonius, nailed forever in his eavesdropping pose, poor spy who could cast very little light. You do nothing right, Hamlet: you have not appeased your father's shade and you have orphaned the maiden you loved. Your character meant you for abstract mental speculation: it is no accident that the *Page of Coins* portrays you absorbed in the contemplation of a circular drawing: perhaps the mandala, diagram of an ultraterrestrial harmony.

Even our less contemplative fellow guest, otherwise known as the *Queen of Swords* or Lady Macbeth, at the sight of *The Hermit*'s card seems distraught: perhaps she sees there another ghostly apparition, the hooded shade of the butchered Banquo, advancing with difficulty along the corridors of the castle, to sit down uninvited at the place of honor at the banquet, shaking his gory locks into the soup. Or else she recognizes her husband in person, Macbeth, who has murdered sleep: by the lantern's glow in the night he visits the guests' rooms, hesitating like a mosquito who dislikes staining the pillowcases. My hands are of your color, but I shame to wear a heart so white!, his wife taunts and drives him, but this does not mean she is so much worse than he: they have shared the roles like a devoted couple, marriage is the encounter of two egoisms that grind each other reciprocally and from which spread the cracks in the foundations of civilized society, the pillars of public welfare stand on the viper's eggshells of private barbarity.

And yet we have seen that in *The Hermit*, with far more verisimilitude, King Lear has recognized himself, outcast and mad, roaming in search of the angelic Cordelia (there, *Temperance* is another lost card, and it is all his fault, this time), the daughter he failed to understand and unjustly drove out while lending credence to the lying treachery of Regan and Goneril. With daughters, whatever a father does is wrong: authoritarian or

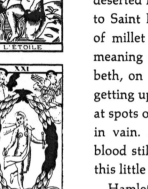

permissive, parents can never expect to be thanked. The generations stare at each other grimly, they speak only to misunderstand each other, to trade blame for growing up unhappy and dying disappointed.

Where has Cordelia got to? Perhaps without any other refuge or clothes to cover herself, she has fled to these deserted heaths, drinking water from the ditches, and as to Saint Mary the Egyptian, the birds bring her grains of millet for her nourishment. This then could be the meaning of the Arcanum *The Star*, in which Lady Macbeth, on the contrary, recognizes herself, sleepwalking, getting up naked at night with her eyes closed but gazing at spots of blood on her hands, as she toils to wash them, in vain. It takes more than that! Here's the smell of blood still. All the perfumes of Arabia will not sweeten this little hand.

Hamlet opposes this interpretation. In his tale he has reached the point (the Arcanum *The World*) where Ophelia loses her mind, burbles nonsense and jingles, wanders through the fields girt with garlands—crow-flowers, nettles, daisies, and long purples that liberal shepherds give a grosser name, but our cold maids do call dear departed's member—and to continue his story he needs that very card, Arcanum Seventeen, in which Ophelia is seen on the bank of a stream, bent toward the glassy and sticky current that in an instant will drown her, staining her hair a moldy green.

Hidden among the graves of the cemetery, Hamlet thinks about *Death*, holding up the jawless skull of Yorick the jester. (This, then, is the roundish object the *Page of Coins* has in his hand!) Where the professional *Fool* is dead, the destructive folly that was reflected in him and found its release through ritual formulas becomes mingled with the language and actions of princes and subjects, unprotected even against themselves. Hamlet already knows that wherever he turns, he collects miscreants; do they believe him incapable of killing? Why, that is the only thing he succeeds in doing! The trouble is that he always strikes mistaken targets: when you kill, you always kill the wrong man.

Two Swords are crossed in a duel: they seem identical, but one is sharp, the other dull, one is poisoned, the other aseptic. However things go, the young are always the first to cut out one another's guts; Laertes and Hamlet, whom a kinder fate would have seen brothers-in-law, are now reciprocal murderer and victim. In the *Cup* King Claudius has thrown a pearl which is a poison-tablet for his nephew: "Gertrude, do not drink!" But the Queen is thirsty. It is too late! Too late, Hamlet's sword runs the king through, the fifth act is already ending.

For all three tragedies the advance of a victorious king's *Chariot* of war marks the fall of the curtain. Fortinbras of Norway lands on the pale Baltic island, the palace is silent, the warrior enters among the marble walls: why, it is a morgue! There lying dead is the entire royal family of Denmark! O proud, snobbish *Death!* What feast is toward in thine eternal cell that thou so many princes at a shot so bloodily hast struck, leafing through the Almanach de Gotha with thy scythe-paper-knife?

No, it is not Fortinbras: it is the King of France, Cordelia's husband, who has crossed the channel to support Lear and is closely besieging the army of Gloucester's Bastard, contended by the two rival and perverse queens, but he will not be in time to free the mad king and his daughter from their cage, shut up there to sing like birds and laugh at gilded butterflies. For the first time there is a bit of peace in the family: if the murderer would delay only a few minutes. But instead he is punctual, hangs Cordelia, and is killed by Lear, who cries: Why should a dog, a horse, a rat have life and thou no breath at all? And Kent, faithful Kent, can only wish for him: Break, heart, I prithee, break!

Unless it is neither the King of Norway nor the King of France, but the legitimate heir of the throne of Scotland usurped by Macbeth. His chariot advances at the head of the English army, and finally Macbeth is forced to say: I 'gin to be aweary of *The Sun*, and wish the syntax o' *The World* were now undone, that the playing cards were shuffled, the folios' pages, the mirror-shards of the disaster.

Note

Note

This book is made first of pictures—the tarot playing cards—and secondly of written words. Through the sequence of the pictures stories are told, which the written word tries to reconstruct and interpret.

The tarots are ancient cards for games and for fortune-telling, popular especially in France and in Italy. The deck consists of seventy-eight cards. Besides the ten numeral cards and the four court cards (*King, Queen, Knight, Page*) for each of the four suits (*Cups, Coins, Clubs, Swords*), there are twenty-one tarots proper (also called the Major Arcana), plus *The Fool*.

Tarots have inspired a vast tradition of cartomancy, based on various interpretations: symbolic, astrological, cabalistic, alchemistic. There are few traces of all this in the present book, where the cards are "read" in the most simple and direct fashion: by observing what the picture portrays and establishing a meaning, which varies according to the sequence of cards into which each individual card is inserted.

The book is made up of two texts, *The Castle of Crossed Destinies* and *The Tavern of Crossed Destinies*. The former was published for the first time in *Tarots: The Visconti Pack in Bergamo and New York* by the publisher Franco Maria Ricci of Parma in 1969 (the same publisher has now, in 1976, brought out an English-language edition). This volume reproduces in color and in the original dimensions the tarots painted by Bonifacio Bembo for the Dukes of Milan around the middle of the fifteenth century. The surviving originals of these miniatures are now divided between the Accademia Carrara in Bergamo and the Morgan Library in New York. This volume reproduces eight of them.

The small black-and-white illustrations throughout the text are based on the highly refined miniatures of Bembo, but they obviously do not mean to take their place. Some cards of the Bembo deck have been lost, including two that are very important for my stories: *The Devil* and *The Tower*. At the places where these cards are mentioned in my text, I was unable to place the corresponding illustrations in the margin.

In *The Castle*, the tarots that make up each story are arranged in a double file, horizontal or vertical, and are crossed by three further double files of tarots (horizontal or vertical) which make up other stories. The result is a general pattern (see page 40) in which you can "read" three stories horizontally and three stories vertically, and in addition, each of these sequences of cards can also be "read" in reverse, as another tale. Thus we have a total of twelve stories.

The central axes of this pattern present episodes inspired by the *Orlando Furioso* of Lodovico ("The Tale of Roland Crazed with Love" and "The Tale of Astolpho on the Moon"). The poem *Orlando Furioso* was written during the first half of the sixteenth century, almost half a century after Bembo's miniatures, but it was born from that same civilization of the Italian courts of the Renaissance.

The second part of the book, *The Tavern*, is similarly composed, with reference to the widely diffused, popular printed tarots, still sold in France today. These are the *Ancien Tarot de Marseille* of the firm of Grimaud, reproducing a deck printed in the eighteenth century (but based certainly on drawings from the previous century). Unlike the painted tarots, these cards lend themselves to reduced printed reproduction, losing none of their connotations, only their colors.

The Marseilles tarots are used in France especially for cartomancy, and they have had a considerable literary renown, particularly since the surrealist period. Very similar to the Marseilles deck are the tarots used in Italy as popular playing cards, in both the North and the South.

There are some variants between the French and the Italian names of the cards. *La Maison-Dieu* is the mysterious French name for the card called in Italian *La Torre* (*The Tower*). *Le Jugement* is known as *L'Angelo* (*The Angel*). *L'Amoureux* may be called *L'Amore* (*Love*) or *Gli Amanti* (*The Lovers*). From the singular *L'Etoile* the name shifts to the plural *Le Stelle*. I have followed whichever nomenclature best suited the situation. The first tarot has an obscure name in both languages: *Le Bateleur*, *Il Bagatto*. As a rule it is interpreted as *The Juggler* or *The Magician*.

In *The Tavern* too the sequence of the tarots composes stories, and the seventy-eight cards spread out on the table form a general pattern (see page 98) in which the various tales intersect. But whereas in *The Castle* the

cards making up the individual tales are in clearly defined horizontal or vertical rows, in *The Tavern* they
form blocks with more irregular outlines, superimposed
in the central area of the general pattern, where cards
that appear in almost all the tales are concentrated.

I publish this book to be free of it: it has obsessed me
for years. I began by trying to line up tarots at random,
to see if I could read a story in them. "The Waverer's
Tale" emerged; I started writing it down; I looked for
other combinations of the same cards; I realized the
tarots were a machine for constructing stories; I thought
of a book, and I imagined its frame: the mute narrators,
the forest, the inn; I was tempted by the diabolical idea
of conjuring up all the stories that could be contained in
a tarot deck.

I thought of constructing a kind of crossword puzzle
made of tarots instead of letters, of pictographic stories
instead of words. I wanted each of the stories to have a
coherent significance, and I wanted them to afford me
pleasure in writing them—or in rewriting them, if they
were already classic stories. I succeeded with the Visconti
tarots because I first constructed the stories of Roland
and Astolpho, and for the other stories I was content to
put them together as they came, with the cards laid
down. I could have followed the same method with the
Marseilles tarots, but I was unwilling to sacrifice any of
the narrative possibilities I was offered by these cards,
so crude and mysterious. The Marseilles tarots continued
giving me ideas, and every tale tended to attract all the
cards to itself. I had already written "The Waverer,"
which required many cards; I had in mind a Shakespear-

ean *pastiche* with Hamlet, Macbeth, King Lear; I didn't want to lose Faust, Parsifal, Oedipus, and the many other famous stories that I saw appear and disappear among the tarots, and also stories that had come to me somewhat accidentally: but all culminated in the same cards, the most dramatic and significant ones.

And so I spent whole days taking apart and putting back together my puzzle; I invented new rules for the game, I drew hundreds of patterns, in a square, a rhomboid, a star design; but some essential cards were always left out, and some superfluous ones were always there in the midst. The patterns became so complicated (they took on a third dimension, becoming cubes, polyhedrons) that I myself was lost in them.

To escape from this impasse I gave up patterns and resumed writing the tales that had already taken shape, not concerning myself with whether or not they would find a place in the network of the others. But I felt that the game had a meaning only if governed by ironclad rules; an established framework of construction was required, conditioning the insertion of one story in the others. Without it, the whole thing was gratuitous.

There was another fact: not all the stories I succeeded in composing visually produced good results when I set myself to writing them down. There were some that sparked no impulse in the writing, and I had to eliminate them because they would have lowered the tension of the style. Then there were others that passed the test and immediately acquired the cohesive strength of the written word which, once written, will not be budged.

Suddenly, I decided to give up, to drop the whole thing; I turned to something else. It was absurd to waste any more time on an operation whose implicit possibilities I had by now explored completely, an operation that made sense only as a theoretical hypothesis. A month went by, perhaps a whole year, and I thought no more about it. Then all of a sudden, it occurred to me that I could try again in a different way, more simple and rapid, with guaranteed success. I began making patterns again, correcting them, complicating them. Again I was trapped in this quicksand, locked in this maniacal obsession. Some nights I woke up and ran to note a decisive correction, which then led to an endless chain of shifts. On other nights I would go to bed relieved at having found the perfect formula; and the next morning, on waking, I would tear it up. Even now, with the book in galleys, I continue to work over it, take it apart, rewrite. I hope that when the volume is printed I will be outside it once and for all. But will this actually happen?

I would like to add that for a certain time it was my intention to write also a third part for this book. At first I wanted to find a third tarot deck fairly different from the other two. But then, instead of going on raving over the same medieval-Renaissance symbols, I thought of creating a sharp contrast, repeating an analogous operation with modern visual material. But what is the tarots' contemporary equivalent as the portrayal of the collective unconscious mind? I thought of comic strips, of the most dramatic, adventurous, frightening ones: gangsters, terrified women, spacecraft, vamps, war in the air, mad scientists. I thought of complementing *The Tavern* and *The Castle* with a similar frame, *The Motel of Crossed Destinies*. Some people who have survived a mysterious catastrophe find refuge in a half-destroyed motel, where only a scorched newspaper page is left, the comics page. The survivors, who have become dumb in their fright, tell their stories by pointing to the drawings, but without following the order of each strip, moving from one strip to another in vertical or diagonal rows.

I went no further than the formulation of the idea as I have just described it. My theoretical and expressive interests had moved off in other directions. I always feel the need to alternate one type of writing with another, completely different, to begin writing again as if I had never written anything before.

CPSIA information can be obtained at www.ICGtesting.com
Printed in the USA
LVOW13s2307300414

383970LV00002B/372/P

9 780156 154550